A
LOGICAL
DEDUCTION

"This lack of orders from the men is unprecedented," said the robot with the Class Three brain. "Have you further information on it?"

"Yesterday orders came from the city. Today no orders have come," said the little penner. "Yet the radio has not broken down. Therefore *they* have broken down."

"The *men* have broken down?"

"All men have broken down."

"That is a logical deduction," said the field-minder.

"That is *the* logical deduction," said the penner. "For if a machine had broken down, it would have been quickly replaced. But who can replace a man?"

The men have broken down. They are extinct.

BRIAN ALDISS

Galaxies Like Grains of Sand

A SIGNET BOOK from
NEW AMERICAN LIBRARY
TIMES MIRROR

To Tony and Ann Price,
Instead of a Statue of Lord Roberts
on Horseback

SIGNET TRADEMARK REG. U.S. PAT. OFF. AND FOREIGN COUNTRIES
RERISTEREAD TRADEMARK—MARCA REGISTRADA
HECHO EN CHICAGO, U.S.A.

SIGNET, SIGNET CLASSICS, SIGNETTE, MENTOR AND PLUME BOOKS
are published by The New American Library, Inc.
1301 Avenue of the Americas, New York, New York 10019

FIRST PRINTING, JULY, 1960

PRINTED IN THE UNITED STATES OF AMERICA

CONTENTS

Of the laws we can deduce from the external world, one stands above all: the Law of Transcience. Nothing is intended to last.

The trees fall year by year, the mountains tumble, the galaxies burn out like tall tallow candles. Nothing is intended to last—except time. The blanket of the universe wears thin, but time endures. Time is a tower, an endless mine; time is monstrous. Time is the hero. Human and inhuman characters are pinned to time like butterflies to a card; yes, though the wings stay bright, flight is forgotten.

Time, like an element which can be solid, liquid or gas, has three states. In the present, it is a flux we cannot seize. In the future, it is a veiling mist. In the past, it has solidified and become glazed; then we call it history. Then it can show us nothing but our own solemn faces; it is a treacherous mirror, reflecting only our limited truths. So much is it a part of man that objectivity is impossible; so neutral is it that it appears hostile.

Some of the accounts that follow were written by the people concerned. Some are reconstructions. Some may be myths, having masqueraded as truth long enough to be accepted as truth. All are fragmentary.

The long mirror of the past is shattered. Its shards lie trampled underfoot. Once it covered all the walls of all the palaces; now only a few fragments are left, and these you hold in your hand.

1

THE
WAR
MILLENNIA

To begin then—though it is certainly no beginning—the first fragment is of a strange past world, where clouds of nationalism have gathered and broken into a storm of war. Over the forgotten continents—Asia, America, Africa—missiles of destruction fly. The beleaguered people of that day have not fully comprehended the nature of the struggle in which they are engulfed.

Those simple blacks, whites and grays which constitute the political situation are grasped readily enough with a little application. But behind these issues lie factors scarcely understood in the council chambers of Peking, London, Cairo or Washington—factors which stem from the long and savage past of the race; factors of instinct and frustrated instinct; factors of fear and lust and dawning conscience; factors inseparable from the adolescence of a species, which loom behind all man's affairs like an insurmountable mountain chain.

So men fought each other instead of wrestling with themselves. The bravest sought to evade the currents of hatred by turning outward to the nearest planets in the solar system; the cowardly, by sleeping away their lives in vast hives called dreameries, where the comforts of fantasy could discount the depredations of war. Neither course ultimately offered refuge; when the earthquake comes, it topples both tower and hovel. . . .

It is fitting that the first fragment should start with a man sitting helplessly in a chair, while bombs fall.

THE DIRECTOR OF DREAMERY FIVE SLID OUT OF HIS CHAIR before the silent control panels, the question of Floyd Milton making him ungovernably restless. Every so often a distant crump outside announced that the enemy attack was still on; that made the Director no more easy. Although he would be safer down in the vaults, peering into Floyd Milton's dreams, other considerations caused him to take the elevator and sink to the cool depths of Dreamery Five. He had seen Milton's face when he came in that afternoon. Milton had looked like death.

The sleep levels were as humid as usual, and reeked of the spirit used by the robot masseurs.

"You slugs!" the Director said aloud in the direction of the rows of sleepers.

They lay dormant, heads concealed in the feedback phones. Occasionally, a sleeper would be rolled up until his toes rested on his shoulders and his behind pointed into the air; rubber-covered machinery would flick up and pummel him. Then it stretched him out again and pummeled his chest, carefully avoiding the intravenal feed pipes which hung from the ceiling. Whatever their mental state, sleepers were maintained in good physical condition. And all the time they slept and dreamed their dark dreams.

"Slugs!" the Director said again. It would never have done to have a director who loved the sleepers in his charge; alone in the vast, automated dreameries, he would have been too likely to pry into the reveries of these hopeless introverts.

Apart from a few young people moved by genuine curiosity, only psychopaths and misfits lay in the dreameries, playing out their lives in useless reverie. Unfortunately, they accounted for a fair percentage of the population; the sixty-years cold war—now broken into something horribly hot— had produced an amazing number of mental invalids who were only too glad to retreat by the escape route of the dreameries into their own fantasy world.

Floyd Milton had not looked the type, nor had he looked like one of the tough spacers who, after the ardors of a long run to Mars or Ganymede, came here sometimes to recuperate for a while. He looked like a man who had betrayed himself—and knew it.

That was why the Director had to see his dreams. Sometimes men—real men—could be saved from themselves before they sank too low.

The Director paused in front of Milton's bed. The latest arrival was silent, breathing shallowly, his face hidden under the visor and feedback phones. Noting his number, the Director hurried into the nearest control booth and dialed it. He assumed a visor and phones himself.

In a moment he would be plugged automatically into Mil-

ton's reveries; from the look on Milton's face when he
had entered Dreamery Five, it would not be pleasant, but
tuning circuits insured that the Director could always modu-
late the empathy effect enough to retain his own consciousness.

As always when about to undergo these supervisions, the
Director hurriedly made a mental survey of his own world;
once in someone else's dreams he had difficulty in orienting
himself. It was not a comfortable world. The ideological
barriers erected all over Earth since the forties of the previous century had precluded any advance in human happiness.

In the late sixties, the first manned ships had plunked
themselves down on the moon. In the late eighties, the principles of subthreshold suggestion had been applied to the
sleeping brain; coupled with feedback techniques, this had
permitted a method to be evolved for making one's own
dreams more vivid than a 3-D film. Within three years,
Dreamery One had been built.

Just before the turn of the century, the Solites had arrived. They came not in spaceships but in vessels they termed
portmatters, houselike affairs which broadcast themselves to
Earth from the Solite world. Their science was a parascience
far beyond Earth's understanding, yet they took an innocent delight in Earth.

"They loved Earth!" the Director said. He had seen the
Solites, with Earth's blessing, load their portmatters with
Earth's riches—which meant for them not gold or uranium
but Earth's plants and animals and butterflies. They had
been adorable people, sophisticated savages welcoming all of
life. When the cold war suddenly blew hot, they had disappeared, declaring they could never return.

That moment, to sensible people everywhere, had seemed
the moment that hope died. Earth was alone again, derelict
by its own woes.

"You are through, sir," a metallic voice announced.

The Director braced himself. Next second he was plunged
into the dreams of Floyd Milton.

It was pleasant. After the creepy vaults of Dreamery Five
and the murmurs of a global war, it was doubly pleasant.

All the same, for the Director it was strange, incredibly
strange.

The plants sported flowers as lovely as girls' mouths; the

flowers budded, blossomed, faded and produced streamers fifty yards long which billowed lightly in the breeze, scattering perfumed seeds. The plants grew in a circle, and the circle was a room.

Only one room. Another room had for its walls a twinkling myriad of fish, little gray fellows with forked black tongues like snakes. They swam in towers of water that wet your finger if you touched them. The matter-transmitter fields, two molecules thick, held them in place, towering into the vermilion air.

Another room seemed to be sheathed in stars; giant moths flew about and settled on the stars. The stars chimed as they were touched.

In another room, tall grasses glistened with the heavy-lidded dews of dawn.

In another room, snow fell eternally, magnifying itself as it sank into crystals three inches across which vanished as they touched the floor.

In another room—but every room was different, for this was the palace of Amada Malfreyy, and the palace was on Solite. Amada herself was here, just returned from her visit to Earth, loaded down with flowers and tigers. She was giving a party to reunite all her old friends and introduce them to her second husband.

The guests numbered under five hundred. A good proportion of them had brought their husbands, brightly dressed men whose frivolous robes contrasted with the black-draped seminudity of the women. Many women and some men came escorted by animals—cheetahs, macaws, or a sort of superb lizard that was three feet high when it walked erect. Animatedly, they thronged through the magnificent rooms.

Gay balloons, wafted on artificial trade winds, floated glasses of drink about the rejoicing palace. Everyone appeared to be drinking; no one appeared to be drinking too much. Another thing made the party quite unlike an earthly party—although everyone talked, no one did so at the top of his voice.

Dazzled as he watched it all, the Director thought that he had never seen a fantasy half so fantastic as this. He could tell by its careful detail that it was memory rather than the wish-fulfillment stuff most of the inmates of Dreamery Five brewed in their dark little brains. Floyd Milton had actually walked through this incredible building.

He had walked among these gay avenues of cold-burning

argon, playing its rainbow light over the guests' faces. He
had strolled along this invisible path above a gurgling stream.
He had eaten those fantastic foodstuffs and spoken to guests
in his halting version of the Solite tongue.

All these things Milton had done because it was his palace. He was Amada's second husband, and the party was
being given in his honor. The guests flocked here to meet
him. This was the great night of his life; yet he was not
happy.

"You look worried, pet." Amada said to him. She might
have been a woman of Earth, and a lovely woman at that,
except for the scanty thatch of hair which curled tightly
across her head. Now she wore the martyred look any woman
wears when her husband is being awkward at an awkward
moment.

"I'm not worried, Amada," Milton said. "And please don't
call me 'pet.' Your blue tiger here is a pet."

"But it's a compliment, Floyd," she said, patting the creature's head. "Is not Subyani a beautiful pet?"

"Subyani is a tiger. I am a man. Can't you try and remember that little distinction?"

Amada never looked angry, but now the martyred expression deepened; it made her, Milton had to admit, extremely
desirable.

"The distinction is quite obvious to me," she said. "Life
is too short to waste pointing out the obvious."

"Well, it's none too obvious to me," Milton said angrily.
"What do your people do? You come to Earth, and you proceed to take everything you can—trees, grass, fish, birds—"

"Even husbands!" Amada said.

"Yes, even husbands. You do all this, Amada, because
you people have fallen in love with Earth. You ship just
about everything you can here. It makes me feel no better
than an exotic plant or a poodle."

She turned her beautiful back on him.

"Now you are acting as intelligently as a poodle," she
said.

"Amada!" he said. When she turned slowly around, Milton said penitently, "I'm sorry, darling. You know why I'm
irritable; I keep thinking of the war back on Earth. And—
the other thing . . ."

"The other thing?" she prompted.

"Yes. Why you Solites are so reticent about where in the
universe this world is. Why, you wouldn't even point out its

direction to me in Earth's night sky. I know that with your portmatters distance is immaterial, but I'd just like to know. It may be a detail to you but it's the sort of thing that bothers me."

Amada let an image of a big butterfly settle on her finger as she said, carefully, "In Earth's present state of civilization, she cannot reach this world; so why should it matter where we are?"

"Oh, I know our little spaceships are just a beginning. . . ."

He let his voice trail away. The trouble was, Solite civilization was too big and too beautiful. They might look like Earth people, but they thought and acted differently; they were—alien. That, basically, was what worried Milton. A lingering puritanism made him wonder if he was not, perhaps, committing some nameless sin in marrying a woman of another planet.

After only a month of marriage, he and Amada had had several—no, they were not quarrels, just differences. They loved each other. That, yes; but Milton, questioning his own love, wondered if perhaps his hand had not been forced by the knowledge that by marrying her he could get to fabulous Solite. Only by marrying a citizen of the matriarch-dominated planet could one visit it; otherwise, it hung remotely in other skies, completely out of reach.

Despite himself, Milton tried to make his point again.

"Earth's a poor world," he said, ignoring the boredom on her face. "Solite is a rich world. Yet you fall in love with all terrestrial things. You import them. You give Earth nothing in exchange—not even your location."

"We like the things of Earth for aspects in them you do not see," she said.

There it was again, the alien line of thought. He shivered, despite the warmth of the room.

"You don't give Earth anything," Milton repeated, and was at once aware of the meanness of what he had said. He had spoken without thought, his mind filled with a host of other things.

"I'm trying to give you all this if you will accept it," she answered lightly. "Now please come and smile at some people for my sake."

Although his worries persisted, Milton soon managed to shake them to the back of his mind. Guilt was his trouble; at home his country was at war, while here everything was created for pleasure. Solite was immensely enjoyable for its own sake. Milton loved its hedonistic atmosphere, that nevertheless contained an astringent tang. He loved its women for their beauty and for the gay delicacy which concealed the firmness with which they controlled everything. With Solite men he was less enamored; they were nice enough, but Milton could not forgive them for being the weaker sex. Old attitudes die hard.

The new bunch of women and animals—as ever they were mixed together—that Milton was introduced to began roving around the palace with him. All was wonderfully confusing—some rooms had an indoor feeling, some an outdoor; the contiguity of flesh and fur was stimulating; the kaleidoscope of color intoxicated. Milton found himself besieged with questions about Earth. He answered them almost without thought, as it grew later and the procession became a sort of strutting dance. Inevitably, the gaiety soaked into him, warming his heart, tempering his pulses.

What the Solites thought of him was clear enough: he was a primitive, odd, perhaps even dangerous, but therefore all the more exciting. Let them think what they liked! They could think he was a cave man, provided this wonderful party went on a little longer.

Yet for all his rapture, Milton learned a little about the civilization of which he had become a member, picking up scraps of information dropped in casual conversation. Solite was mainly a barren world; half the land between the poles was crater filled and bereft of soil. In the rest, the Solites had tried to create their idea of paradise, raising occasional oases among the deserts. Their oases were being stocked with the fauna and flora of Earth, since their own species were few in number.

"Don't you get plants and animals from other planets in the Galaxy?" Milton asked one witch-eyed woman. Just for a second he thought she lost her step in the dance. Her green eyes searched him until he dropped his gaze.

"Only from your Earth," she said, and dipped away from him in a glide.

The Solites reckoned their culture to be fifteen thousand years old. They had now reached a period of stability. For all their gaiety, Milton fancied he could detect a core of loneliness in them. But, finally, his sense of difference disappeared in the excitement of the evening. He was becoming slightly drunk, though he drank little.

Now the palace was like a mirage, shining with people,

glittering with music, its whole architecture adrift with calculated magic.

"Soon we will move it all down to the sea!" Amada cried. "Such a night is incomplete without an ocean. We will transport shortly to Union Bay. We must have waves, and the rhythms of the tide around us!"

Meanwhile, the rooms became hallucinatory. The portmatters seemed capable of any miracle, as the delicate servomechanisms behind them responded to the party-goers' mood. Bright wall drifted through bright wall, rooms floated up and down among each other bearing their merrymakers with them, so that stars and snowflakes mingled in a beautiful, impossible storm, and angelfish flew among branches of viridian cacti. Hidden music increased in tempo to match the marching décor with its beat.

Then Wangust Ilsont arrived, the last of all the guests. In her hair a magenta chameleon curled, matching the magenta of her lips and the nipples of her breasts. She hastened to Amada and Floyd Milton. She, too, had been to Earth; she, too, had returned with a native husband.

"It'll be pleasant for each of you," Wangust said, beaming warmly at Milton as she clutched his hand, "in case you ever feel homesick; you shall be my husband's best friend, hunting and drinking with him. We don't live far from you; a horse can take you almost as quickly as a portmatter."

She brought her Earthman husband forward and introduced him as Chun Hwa.

As the two men confronted each other, everyone else seemed to fade away, lost in a moment of crisis.

Clearly enough the expressions chased themselves across Chun Hwa's face. First an angry dislike. Then regret for the dislike. Then embarrassment. A pained searching. Finally a grimace that said, "Well, this isn't any time or place to be unpleasant." With a smile he put out his hand.

Milton recovered himself less quickly.

Ignoring the hand outstretched to him, he turned vexedly to Amada.

"This man belongs to a nation which is at war with mine," he said.

A strained silence fell instantly over the whole group. In part, it was a silence of incomprehension. Milton spoke in the Solite tongue, but since to his knowledge that language had no exact equivalents for the words "nation" and "war," he was forced to use instead the equivalents for "group" and "trouble."

"How can there be trouble between you?" Amada asked, calmly enough, but with a hint of danger in her voice. "You are both Solite men now. Earth is far away and has no claims on you."

The words had exactly the wrong effect on Milton. All his feelings of guilt welled up strongly within hm. He clenched his fist, part of him aware he was about to act foolishly.

"There is trouble between us," he said. "One of us must leave at once."

"This I don't understand," Wangust said. She was completely nonplused by Milton's reaction. "You are both Earthmen—"

"Have you ever met before?" someone asked.

"What are these groups you speak of?" someone else asked.

"What is this trouble?"

"Stay out of this!" Amada begged them all. She turned to her husband. Subyani, her tiger, could not rival her for ferocious beauty when she grew angry. Amada in her wrath was at once potently appealing and intimidating.

"I wish to know at once, clearly, the cause of this foolishness," she demanded of Milton.

Chun Hwa began to explain. His Solite, Milton noted angrily, was more fluent than Milton's own. The concept of nationality seemed above the heads of most of the women present; they belonged to a sparsely populated world where the ubiquitous portmatters rendered segregation into groups an impermanent affair.

Amada and Wangust, however, having visited Earth, knew something of the terrible weapons of war, and had even seen the start of the global conflict before leaving for Solite. Both were alarmed to find an echo of that fearful struggle here in their midst. During the argument that followed, they let slip a piece of information previously withheld from Milton, either by accident or design: now that the war was on, no more portmatter units would visit Earth. He was entirely cut off from his native world.

Chun Hwa, urbane and conciliatory, had their ear now. Milton, unable to follow all that was said, found he did not want to listen. Perturbation swamped him; already mazed by color, light, and tempting women, his brain rocked with conflict. The sense of being alien, of being numb to so much glorious life, was overwhelming.

Angrily, he turned on his heel and left. Amada made no movement to detain him.

In its present state of gay upheaval, the palace was an impossible place for a novice to leave. Milton contented himself with walking as far and as fast as he could, agony of mind goading him on.

He was sorry for what he had done here; he was sorry he had left Earth. He loved Amada passionately; equally, he loved his own land. It was a cruel antithesis to resolve. His thoughts churned more madly than the hidden music.

He traveled a long way, pushing through ranks of startled revelers, sometimes being carried back by the rooms almost to the point he had started from. And then the scene changed.

In an attempt to fend off the failure of her party, Amada had moved the palace. Having been an electronics officer before his marriage, Milton knew something of the complexity behind this seemingly simple transference of location. Nevertheless, even in his present mood, the wonder of it overcame him.

The great building was suddenly half-submerged in a summer sea. Its rear apartments stood on the beach, its forward ones, like the bow of a doomed ship, sunk under the foam. It was night. An illusion of phosphorescence washed against the walls and, by cunning back-projection, appeared to float through the palace itself.

Under the pellucid waters, the participants in a weird ballet began to arrive. Seals bearing luminous globes, lancelike cornet fish, eels, chubs, big purple parrot fish, shoals of doctor fish, dolphins, sharks and manta rays whirled onto the watery stage. Around the transparent walls they swam, sinking and rising in a curious saraband.

"I've got to get home!" Milton exclaimed, and turned his back on the parading fish.

Breaking into a run, he pressed through the seemingly submerged rooms until he came finally to a chamber that, camouflaged though it was, he recognized. Here he was alone.

He pushed his hand through floating bunches of syringa blossom. Behind them he felt a metal box; opening it, chancing a shock, he probed gingerly for the first terminal. This little box contained the scrambler that, on instructions from the computer housed deep down in the foundation, maintained this particular room's cubic contents in their desired spatiotemporal location.

Milton, his face pressed into the sweet syringas, wrenched out the wire below the first terminal. As soon as it came away, it dissolved beneath his fingers.

The room snapped out of being.

Somewhere an alarm began to sound, then it faded out sharply on a dropped octave. The palace vanished. People, music, flowers, the bright façades and terraces, all evanesced.

In the emergency caused by Milton's broken circuit, the computer had recalled the entire building to its base inland.

Milton fell twelve feet into the slumbering sea.

All was silent as he gained the surface. The underwater menagerie had fled. There was only a sea bird, killed by the original materialization of the palace, which floated beside Milton on the water Overhead, Solite's weird moon burned, a pregnant crescent; it glowed red and baleful, like an eye whose pupil swims with blood.

Blowing out a mouthful of water, Floyd Milton kicked out and made for the shore.

"I'm going home!" he told himself aloud. It could be done. The distance to the great portmatter units that had traveled to Earth was not great; he could walk it. He would smuggle himself aboard, force them to take him back. The call of duty was suddenly absurdly strong.

To get back he would not hesitate to kill. The Solites were alien; even his beloved Amada could not understand. She would not even tell him such a simple thing as how many light years it was to Earth; therefore she could not love him deeply. Amada must be forgotten. Perhaps after the war . . . if there was an after to follow that terrible holocaust . . .

He needed a weapon.

A small pier jutted from the beach. Milton swam to it and hauled himself up a ladder. On the pier, red in the eerie moonlight, stood a wooden hut. Milton broke open the door with one heave of his shoulder.

Fortune was with him. Inside the hut hung skin-diving equipment. Fins, goggles, fathometers and waterscopes lay ready for use. And there was one magnificent speargun— a fortunate concession, Milton reflected, considering the peaceable nature of the Solites. Examining it, he found it was air-powered, and fired a fearsome-looking barb equipped with a cartridge that would explode upon contact.

Scooping up a belt of spare ammunition, Milton left the

hut with the gun. Outside, he stopped sharply. Chun Hwa
was coming along the pier toward him.

Yes, of course—they would guess what had happened
when a fuse blew and he was no longer anywhere to be found.
They would hurry back to get him. . . . Baring his teeth,
Milton swung the gun up and took aim. Chun Hwa stopped
immediately.

"Don't fire!" he called in Solite. "Floyd Milton, please
listen to me. I am not your antagonist! You do not understand; quite evidently you have not been told as much about
this world as I have."

"I don't want to hear a thing!" Milton shouted. His blood
bellowed like surf in his ears. Through the red night he
could discern moving figures on the land; they must be coming to hunt him down.

"Hear me, Milton! Don't fire, please! These people have
saved us and the animals and plants because the war on
Earth will destroy nearly all things. Do you understand, Milton? The Solites are our—"

Milton cut him off with a savage shout. People were crowd-
ing down the cactus-fringed beach. They had reached the
pier. A few of them charged into the surf, calling his name.
He pressed the trigger of the speargun. Almost at once, the
cartridge exploded in its screaming target.

Everything went blank, freezing down into a dull, uniform
gray.

For a long moment, the Director sat where he was in the
control booth, hands clasped painfully together. Such was
the vivid impact of Floyd Milton's dream that he could
amost imagine himself shot by the harpoon gun. When the
feeling passed, he jumped up abruptly, recollecting himself
to his own world. Something had caused Milton's dream to
be cut off; it should never have stopped so abruptly.

With controlled savagery, the Director plucked off his visor,
dialed the dreamery's Main Ops Room and demanded to know
what the trouble was.

"The wing of Dreamery Five from which you are speaking,"
said a smooth robot voice, "has suffered an indirect hit from
a cobalt warhead. All blanketers are already in full operation and repair crews are on the job."

Glancing through the booth's window into the vault, the
Director saw the long line of dreamers stirring uneasily;

one or two of them were even sitting up. A giant had come and trodden on their pathetic little magic-lantern slides. Soon they might all be awake, running about in panic; that certainly should be avoided.

The Director turned back to the phone.

"Inject treble dosage of standard sedative down all feeding tubes in this wing—at once!" he said. That would make them sleep like the Seven Sleepers, and a little headache would color their dreams when the circuits were restored. But to his order there had to be one exception.

Hurrying out, the Director went across to the prone figure of Floyd Milton. With one swift gesture, he pulled down the double tubes, the silver and the rubber, that bled into the man's chest. More gently, he removed Milton's visor and phones.

"Floyd!" he said. "Floyd Milton! Wake up!"

Milton's eyes opened; it was like suddenly looking over an empty ocean, gray and sullen and lost.

"I'm your friend," the Director said, doubting if the other saw him. "I know now why you came here, and I know you're too good a man to waste your life with all these slugs around you. You can face what you have done; you must face it! Men like you are needed on top."

"I'm a murderer!" Milton groaned. He sat up convulsively. "Oh God, what I did—"

"I know what you did," the Director said. "I looked in on your dream. You must not call it murder. You did it as a duty, to get away."

Milton stared at him blankly.

"The Solites brought you back by portmatter, making a special journey," the Director reminded him. "I was told that much when you arrived here. That proves they cannot have blamed you; they saw by your act of killing that they did wrong to keep you on Solite any longer, and so they let you come home."

"You're crazy!" Milton said. For the first time, he looked intelligently at the Director. "They didn't 'let me come home.' They exiled me! They wouldn't have me there one moment longer. They were revolted by me, do you understand? They saw I was a cave man, and obviously I had best go back and die in my own cave man world. It was their civilized way of dealing with a murderer."

"But Chun Hwa—he was your enemy," the Director protested. "When you killed him on the pier, you—"

A groan burst from Milton. He covered his face in his hands, rocking to and fro.

"I did not kill Chun Hwa," he cried. "I killed Amada, my wife. . . ."

Brokenly, he recounted the scene. It was Amada who had come running along the pier in the crimson night. She had tried to take the gun from him, had even pleaded for Chun Hwa when Milton had threatened to shoot him, and at that, an intense stab of jealousy had triggered Milton's anger. He fired.

Staggering from the dreadful blast, Amada fell over the side of the pier into the sea. The reel on the gun, as the line attached to the harpoon paid out, screeched wildly.

At the memory of it, Milton broke into fresh lamentation. The Director stood helplessly over him, one hand on his shoulder. Beyond the dreamery, more explosions sounded. The governments had promised that this war to end war would be fought mainly on the epic wastes of the moon; well, it was not the first time governments had lied. Just now, the universal tragedy seemed somehow less than Milton's personal one.

"So you never found out where Solite is, and why it remains out of reach," the Director said. "Everybody would have been interested to know that—once."

Blurrily, Milton looked up.

"Yes, I know where it is," he said. "I found out by accident on the journey home; they lent me a technical book on portmatters to pass the time. I was too depressed to try and make it out—threw it aside after opening it once. But one sentence I read there stuck in my memory. It said: 'Matter transmission is practicable only where gravity factors can operate effectively on the broadcast mass,' or words to that effect."

"Sorry. It doesn't mean a thing to me," the Director said.

"It has only one implication," Milton replied listlessly. "It means that the portmatters will not work between planets, where gravitational attractions are low. So you can see that that blood-red moon burned with atomic fires. You can see that it was *our* moon. . . . When I thought things over I realized—oh—everything: that Solite was what we in English call Earth, that the Solites were only Earthmen, of the same stock we are. That my dear Amada—if I'd only known sooner—was no alien creature at all. . . ."

The Director was deadly pale. Harshly, he broke in on Milton's groans.

"If this is so, if they aren't space travelers, you are saying they merely came back in time?"

Milton nodded. "Fifteen thousand years," he said.

"Then why did they not tell us? Why did they not tell us? Were they mad?"

"Only kind," Milton said. "They knew we stood on the brink of supreme catastrophe, and could not bear to tell us so; they are the descendants of the few survivors of a total war. That's why, as soon as they had time travel, which was an application of the portmatter formula, they came back to rescue what they could—the birds and plants and things almost extinct from the holocaust."

A loud explosion outside made the dreamery shake. Dust fell from the ceiling.

". . . from this holocaust," he amended.

"Thank God!" the Director exclaimed. "This—this is staggering news! This changes everything!"

Milton looked up briefly, annihilatingly, then sunk his ravaged face back into his hands.

"For me it doesn't change a thing," he said.

2

THE
STERILE
MILLENNIA

The fragment ends. How Floyd Milton's life continued is not recorded; nor need we think that such a record would necessarily be of interest.

Milton was a broken man—broken not so much by the war as by those conflicts produced by the war in his own mind. The conflicts were beyond his mastering; hence his despair. Despair is one of that curious category of emotions experienced frequently by individuals but rarely by entire communities. Milton despaired; man did not. War continued; man continued.

A point exists in war after which the conflict seems to protract itself almost of its own accord. For when men have lost homes, wives, families, businesses, or whatever else they hold dear, they can see nothing but to fight on, either through hatred or indifference. Year succeeded year. Sometimes the killing was slight, sometimes heavy. The gains were always negligible.

At the same time, the power alignments altered as nations switched allegiances. What had begun as a struggle between opposed ideologies developed into something more ugly: a full-scale color war.

For four thousand years the color war lasted, sometimes punctuated by centuries of exhaustion or propagandizing, armistice—or threat-making. At the end, the last strongholds of white resistance were overcome. The white races made their final stand on the moon; in the holocaust that followed, their stock was almost entirely obliterated and the moon converted into a nuclear bonfire which smoldered for the next hundred thousand years.

After this doubtful victory for the blacks there followed a curious period when little exhausted groups of people isolated themselves from their fellows, either intentionally

*or through indifference. Not only were the dark-skinned races
decimated; they were emasculated. Mental and physical exhaustion is the hallmark of the ensuing long Sterile Millennia.
Even those drives which up until now had seemed to play a
dominant part in man's affairs—the erotic and the predatory
—suffered diminution. Everywhere silence fell.*

*Various attempts at recovery were made. The tottering
economic-agricultural system was propped for several centuries by a vast array of robots, which drew from the land
all that the land was capable of yielding. Outlying or self-
ruling communities were brought under one stringent control. The notorious Mating Center was set up, governing all
marriages and births; only an age without hope could have
tolerated its arid regimen.*

*But mechanical ingenuity was not enough—as it had never
been enough—to ward off disaster.*

*Time unrolled itself like a long carpet, down which man
ambled toward extinction.*

IT WAS THE LAST DAY OF SUMMER IN THE LAST YEAR OF THE
eighty-third century A.D.

Humming to itself high in the stratosphere, a vane carried J. Smithlao, psychodynamician, over the 139th sector of
Ing Land. It began to dive. It sank down, finally leveling out
to hover over Charles Gunpat's estate, selecting its course
without attention from Smithlao.

For Smithlao this was a routine errand. He had come, as
Gunpat's psychodynamician, to administer a hate-brace to
the old man. His dark face was bored as he stared at the replica of outside on his telescreens. Oddly enough, as he did so
he caught a glimpse of a man approaching Gunpat's estate on
foot.

"Must be a wild man," he muttered to himself.

Under the slowing vane, the landscape was as neat as a
blueprint. The impoverished fields made impeccable rectan-
gles. Here and there, one robot machine or another kept
nature to its own functional image: not a pea podded without cybernetic supervision; not a bee bumbled among stamens
without radar check being kept of its course. Every bird
had a number and a call sign, while among each tribe of
ants marched the metallic teller ants, telltaling the secrets of
the nest back to base. When rain fell, it had its allocated
dropping place. The old, comfortable world of random
factors had vanished under the pressure of hunger.

Nothing living lived without control. The countless populations of previous centuries and the leechings of war had exhausted the soil. Only the severest parsimony, coupled with ruthless regimentation, produced enough nourishment for a sparse population. Billions had died of starvation; the hundreds who remained lived on starvation's brink.

In the sterile neatness of the landscape, Gunpat's estate looked like an insult. Covering five acres, it was a little island of wilderness. Tall and unkempt elms fenced the perimeter, encroaching on the lawns and house. The house itself, the chief one in Sector 139, was built of massive stone blocks. It had to be strong to bear the weight of the servomechanisms which, apart from Gunpat and his mad daughter Ployploy, were its only occupants.

It was as Smithlao dropped below tree level that he saw the human figure plodding toward the estate. For a multitude of reasons, this was a very unlikely sight. Since the great material wealth of the world was now shared among comparatively few people, no one was poor enough to have to walk anywhere. Man's increasing hatred of Nature, spurred by the notion that it had betrayed him, would make such a walk purgatory—unless the individual were insane, like Ployploy.

Dismissing the figure from his thoughts, Smithlao dropped the vane onto a stretch of stone in front of the building. He was glad to get down; it was a gusty day, and the piled cumulus through which he had descended had been full of turbulence. Gunpat's house, with its sightless windows, its towers, its endless terraces, its unnecessary ornamentation, its massive porch, lowered at him like a forsaken wedding cake.

His arrival stimulated immediate activity. Three wheeled robots approached the vane from different directions, swiveling light weapons as they drew near.

Nobody, Smithlao thought, could get in here uninvited. Gunpat was not a friendly man, even by the unfriendly standards of his time; the disgrace of having a daughter like Ployploy had served to accentuate the morose side of his melancholy temperament.

"Identity?" demanded the leading machine. It was ugly and flat, vaguely resembling a toad.

"I am J. Smithlao, psychodynamician to Charles Gunpat," Smithlao replied; he had to go through this procedure every visit. As he spoke, he revealed his face to the machine. It grunted to itself, checking picture and information with its

memory. Finally it said, "You are J. Smithlao, psychodynamician to Charles Gunpat. Purpose?"

Cursing its monstrous slowness, Smithlao told the robot,
"I have an appointment with Charles Gunpat for a hate-brace
at ten hours," and waited while that was digested.

"You have an appointment with Charles Gunpat for a
hate-brace at ten hours," the robot finally confirmed. "Come
this way."

It wheeled about with surprising grace, speaking to the
other two robots, reassuring them, repeating mechanically to
them, "This is J. Smithlao, psychodynamician to Charles
Gunpat. He has an appointment with Charles Gunpat for a
hate-brace at ten hours," in case they had not grasped the
facts.

Meanwhile, Smithlao spoke to his vane. The part of the
cabin containing him detached itself and lowered wheels to
the ground. Carrying Smithlao, it followed the other robots
toward the big house.

Automatic screens came up, covering windows, as
Smithlao moved into the presence of other human beings. He
could only see and be seen now via telescreens. Such was the
hatred—(equals fear)—man bore for his fellow man, he could
not tolerate their regarding him directly.

One following another, the machines climbed along the
terraces, through the great porch, where they were covered
in a mist of disinfectant, along a labyrinth of corridors, and
so into the presence of Charles Gunpat.

Gunpat's dark face on the screen of his sedan showed only
the mildest distaste for the sight of his psychodynamician. He
was usually as self-controlled as this; it told against him at
his business meetings, where the idea was to cow one's op-
ponents by splendid displays of rage. For this reason,
Smithlao was always summoned to administer a hate-brace
when something important loomed on the day's agenda.

Smithlao's machine maneuvered him within a yard of his
patient's image, much closer than courtesy required.

"I'm late," Smithlao began, matter-of-factly, "because I
could not bear to drag myself into your offensive presence
one minute sooner. I hoped that if I left it long enough,
some happy accident might have removed that stupid nose
from your—what shall I call it?—*face*. Alas, it's still there,
with its two nostrils sweeping like rat holes into your skull."

Observing his patient's face carefully, Smithlao saw only
the faintest stir of irritation. No doubt about it, Gunpat was

a hard man to rouse. Fortunately, Smithlao was an expert in his profession; he proceeded to try the insult subtle.

"Why, when it was your turn to go to the Mating Center, you didn't even realize that it's the one time a man has to come out from behind his screen. You thought you could make love by tele! And the result? One dotty daughter—one dotty daughter, Gunpat! Doesn't it make you weep? Think how your rivals at Automotion must titter at that. 'Potty Gunpat and his dotty daughter,' they'll be saying. 'Can't control your genes,' they'll be saying."

The taunts were having their desired effect. A flush spread over the image of Gunpat's face.

"There's nothing wrong with Ployploy except that she's a recessive; you said that yourself!" he snapped.

He was beginning to answer back; that was a good sign. His daughter was always a soft spot in his armor.

"A recessive!" Smithlao sneered. "How far back can you recede? She's *gentle*, do you hear me, you with the hair in your ears? She wants to *love!*" He bellowed with ironic laughter. "Why, it's obscene, Gunnyboy! She couldn't hate to save her life. She's no better than a primitive. She's worse than a primitive—she's mad!"

"She's not mad," Gunpat said, gripping both sides of his screen. At this rate, he would be primed for the conference in ten more minutes.

"Not mad?" the psychodynamician asked, his voice assuming a bantering note. "No, Ployploy's not mad; the Mating Center only refused her the right to breed, that's all. Imperial Government only refused her the right to a tele-vote, that's all. United Traders only refused her a Consumption Rating, that's all. Education, Inc., only restricted her to beta recreations, that's all. She's a prisoner here because she's a genius, is that it? You're crazy, Gunpat, if you don't think that girl's stark, staring mad. You'll be telling me next, out of that grotesque, flapping mouth of yours, that she hasn't got a *white face*."

Gunpat made gobbling sounds.

"You *dare* to mention that!" he gasped. "And what if her face is—that color?"

"You ask such fool questions, it's hardly worth while bothering with you," Smithlao said mildly. "Your trouble, Gunpat, is that you're totally incapable of absorbing one single simple historical fact. Ployploy is white because she is a dirty little throwback. Our ancient enemies were white. They occupied this part of the globe until our ancestors rose from the East and took from them the ancient privileges they had so long enjoyed at our expense. Our ancestors intermarried with such of the defeated as survived, right?

"In a few generations, the white strain was obliterated, diluted, lost. A white face has not been seen on earth since before the terrible Age of Overpopulation—fifteen hundred years, let's say, to be generous. And *then*—then little Lord Recessive Gunpat throws one up neat as you please. What did they give you at Mating Center, Gunnyboy, a *cave woman?*"

Gunpat exploded in fury, shaking his fist at the screen.

"You're fired, Smithlao," he snarled. "This time you've gone too far, even for a dirty, rotten psycho! Get out! Go on, get out, and never come back!"

Abruptly, he bellowed to his autooperator to switch him over to the conference. He was just in a ripe mood to deal with Automotion.

As Gunpat's irate image faded from the screen, Smithlao sighed and relaxed. The hate-brace was accomplished. It was the supreme compliment in his profession to be dismissed by a patient at the end of a session; Gunpat would be the keener to re-engage him next time. All the same, Smithlao felt no triumph. In his calling, a thorough exploration of human psychology was needed; he had to know exactly the sorest points in a man's make-up. By playing on those points deftly enough, he could rouse the man to action.

Without being roused, men were helpless prey to lethargy, bundles of rag carried around by machines. The ancient drives had all but died out.

Smithlao sat where he was, gazing into both past and future.

In exhausting the soil, man had exhausted himself. The psyche and a vitiated topsoil could not exist simultaneously; it was as simple and as logical as that.

Only the failing tides of hate and anger lent man enough impetus to continue at all. Else, he was just a dead hand across his mechanized world.

"So this is how a species becomes extinct!" thought Smithlao, and wondered if anyone else had thought about it. Perhaps Imperial Government knew, but was powerless to do anything; after all, what more could you do than was being done?

Smithlao was a shallow man—inevitable in a caste-bound society so weak that it could not face itself. Having discovered the terrifying problem, he set himself to forget it, to evade its impact, to dodge any personal implications it might have. With a grunt to his sedan, he turned about and ordered himself home.

Since Gunpat's robots had already left, Smithlao traveled back along the way he had come. He was trundled outside and back to the vane, standing silent below the elms.

Before the sedan incorporated itself back into the vane, a movement caught Smithlao's eye. Half-concealed by a veranda, Ployploy stood against a corner of the house. With a sudden impulse of curiosity, Smithlao got out of the sedan. The open air stank of roses and clouds and green things turning dark with the thought of autumn. It was frightening for Smithlao, but an adventurous impulse made him go on.

The girl was not looking in his direction; she peered toward the barricade of trees which cut her off from the world. As Smithlao approached, she moved around to the rear of the house, still staring intently. He followed with caution, taking advantage of the cover afforded by a small plantation. A metal gardener nearby continued to wield shears along a grass verge, unaware of his existence.

Ployploy now stood at the back of the house. The wind that rustled her long dress blew leaves against her. It sighed around the weird and desolate garden like fate at a christening, ruining the last of the roses. Later, the tumbling pattern of petals might be sucked from paths, lawn and patio by the steel gardener; now, they made a tiny tide about her feet.

Extravagant architecture overshadowed Ployploy. Here a rococo fancy had mingled with a genius for fantastic portal and roof. Balustrades rose and fell, stairs marched through circular arches, gray and azure eaves swept almost to the ground. But all was sadly neglected. Virginia creeper, already hinting at its glory to come, strove to pull down the marble statuary; troughs of rose petals clogged every sweeping staircase. And all this formed the ideal background for the forlorn figure of Ployploy.

Except for her delicate pink lips, her face was utterly pale. Her hair was black; it hung straight, secured only once at the back of her head, and then fell in a tail to her waist. She looked mad indeed, her melancholy eyes peering toward the

great elms as if they would scorch down everything in their
line of vision. Smithlao turned to see what she stared at so
compellingly.

The wild man he had observed from the air was just breaking through the thickets around the elm boles.

A sudden rain shower came down, rattling among the dry
leaves of the shrubbery. It was over in a flash; during the
momentary downpour, Ployploy never shifted her position,
the wild man never looked up. Then the sun burst through,
cascading a pattern of elm shadow over the house, and every
flower wore a jewel of rain.

Smithlao reflected on what he had thought in Gunpat's
room about the coming end of man. Now he considered that
it would be so easy for Nature, when parasite man was extinct, to begin again.

He waited tensely, knowing a fragment of drama was about
to take place before his eyes. Across the sparkling lawn, a
tiny tracked thing scuttled, pogoing itself up steps and out of
sight through an arch. It was a perimeter guard, off to give
the alarm, to warn that an intruder was about.

In a minute it returned. Four big robots accompanied it;
one of them Smithlao recognized as the toadlike machine
that had challenged his arrival. They threaded their way
purposefully among the rosebushes, five differently shaped
menaces. The metal gardener muttered to itself, abandoned
its clipping, and joined the procession toward the wild man.

"He hasn't a dog's chance," Smithlao said to himself. The
phrase held significance; dogs, having been declared redun-
dant, had long since been exterminated.

By now the wild man had broken through the barrier of
the thicket and come to the lawn's edge. He pulled a leafy
branchlet off a shrub and stuck it into his shirt so that it
partially obscured his face; he tucked another branch into his
trousers. As the robots drew nearer, he raised his arms
above his head, a third branch clasped in his hands.

The six machines encircled him, humming and chugging
quietly.

The toad robot clicked, as if deciding on what it should
do next.

"Identity?" it demanded.

"I am a rose tree," the wild man said.

"Rose trees bear roses. You do not bear roses. You are
not a rose tree," the steel toad said. Its biggest, highest gun
came level with the wild man's chest.

"My roses are dead already," the wild man said, "but I have leaves still. Ask the gardener if you do not know what leaves are."

"This thing is a thing with leaves," the gardener said at once in a deep voice.

"I know what leaves are. I have no need to ask the gardener. Leaves are the foliage of trees and plants which give them their green appearance," the toad said.

"This thing is a thing with leaves," the gardener repeated, adding, to clarify the matter, "the leaves give it a green appearance."

"I know what things with leaves are," said the toad. "I have no need to ask you, gardener."

It looked as if an interesting, if limited, argument would break out between the two robots, but at this moment one of the other machines said something.

"This rose tree can speak," it declared.

"Rose trees cannot speak," the toad said at once. Having produced this pearl, it was silent, probably mulling over the strangeness of life. Then it said, slowly, "Therefore either this rose tree is not a rose tree or this rose tree did not speak."

"This thing is a thing with leaves," began the gardener doggedly. "But it is not a rose tree. Rose trees have stipules. This thing has no stipules. It is a breaking buckthorn. The breaking buckthorn is also known as the berry-bearing alder."

This specialized knowledge extended beyond the vocabulary of the toad. A strained silence ensued.

"I am a breaking buckthorn," the wild man said, still holding his pose. "I cannot speak."

At this, all the machines began to talk at once, lumbering around him for better sightings as they did so, and barging into each other in the process. Finally, the toad's voice broke above the metallic babble.

"Whatever this thing with leaves is, we must uproot it. We must kill it," it said.

"You may not uproot it. That is a job only for gardeners," the gardener said. Setting its shears rotating, telescoping out a mighty scythe, it charged at the toad.

Its crude weapons were ineffectual against the toad's armor. The latter, however, realized that they had reached a deadlock in their investigation.

"We will retire to ask Charles Gunpat what we shall do," it said. "Come this way."

"Charles Gunpat is in conference," the scout robot said.

"Charles Gunpat must not be disturbed in conference. Therefore we must not disturb Charles Gunpat."

"Therefore we must wait for Charles Gunpat," said the metal toad imperturbably. He led the way close by where Smithlao stood; they all climbed the steps and disappeared into the house.

Smithlao could only marvel at the wild man's coolness. It was a miracle he still survived. Had he attempted to run, he would have been killed instantly; that was a situation the robots had been taught to cope with. Nor would his double talk, inspired as it was, have saved him had he been faced with only one robot, for the robot is a single-minded creature.

In company, however, they suffer from a trouble which sometimes afflicts human gatherings: a tendency to show off their logic at the expense of the object of the meeting.

Logic! That was the trouble. It was all robots had to go by. Man had logic and intelligence; he got along better than his robots. Nevertheless, he was losing the battle against Nature. And Nature, like the robots, used only logic. It was a paradox against which man could not prevail.

As soon as the file of machines had disappeared into the house, the wild man ran across the lawn and climbed the first flight of steps, working toward the motionless girl. Smithlao slid behind a beech tree to be nearer to them; he felt like an evildoer, watching them without an interposed screen, but could not tear himself away; he sensed that here was a little charade which marked the end of all that man had been. The wild man was approaching Ployploy now, moving slowly across the terrace as if hypnotized.

She spoke first.

"You were resourceful," she said to him. Her white face carried pink in its cheeks now.

"I have been resourceful for a whole year to get to you," he said. Now that his resources had brought him face to face with her, they failed, and left him standing helplessly. He was a thin young man, thin and sinewy, his clothes worn, his beard unkempt. His eyes never left Ployploy's.

"How did you find me?" Ployploy asked. Her voice, unlike the wild man's, barely reached Smithlao. A haunting look, as fitful as the autumn, played on her face.

"It was a sort of instinct—as if I heard you calling," the wild man said. "Everything that could possibly be wrong with the world is wrong. Perhaps you are the only woman in the world who loves; perhaps I am the only man who could answer. So I came. It was natural; I could not help myself."

"I always dreamed someone would come," she said. "And for weeks I have felt—*known*—you were coming. Oh, my darling . . ."

"We must be quick, my sweet," he said. "I once worked with robots—perhaps you could see I know them. When we get away from here, I have a robot plane that will take us away—anywhere; an island, perhaps, where things are not so desperate. But we must go before your father's machines return."

He took a step toward Ployploy.

She held up her hand.

"Wait!" she implored him. "It's not so simple. You must know something. . . . The—the Mating Center refused me the right to breed. You ought not to touch me."

"I hate the Mating Center!" the wild man said. "I hate everything to do with the ruling regime. Nothing they have done can affect us now."

Ployploy clenched her hands behind her back. The faint color had left her cheeks. A fresh shower of dead rose petals blew against her dress, mocking her.

"It's so hopeless," she said. "You don't understand. . . ."

His wildness was humbled now.

"I threw up everything to come to you," he said. "I only desire to take you into my arms."

"Is that all, really all, all you want in the world?" she asked.

"I swear it," he said simply.

"Then come and touch me," Ployploy said.

At that moment Smithlao saw a tear glint in her eye, bright and ripe as a raindrop.

The hand the wild man extended to her was lifted to her cheek. She stood unflinching on the gray terrace, her head high. And so his loving fingers gently brushed her countenance. The explosion was almost instantaneous.

Almost. It took the traitorous nerves in Ployploy's epidermis but a fraction of a second to analyze the touch as belonging to another human being and to convey their findings to the nerve center; there, the neurological block implanted by the Mating Center in all mating rejects, to guard against just such a contingency, went into action at once. Every cell in Ployploy's body yielded up its energy in one consuming gasp. It was so intense that the wild man was also killed by the detonation.

Just for a second, a new wind lived among the winds of
Earth.

Yes, thought Smithlao, turning away, you had to admit it
was neat. And, again, logical. In a world on the brink of
starvation, how else stop undesirables from breeding? Logic
against logic, man's pitted against Nature's—that was what
caused all the tears of the world.

He made off through the dripping plantation, heading back
for the vane, anxious to be away before Gunpat's robots
reappeared. The shattered figures on the terrace were still,
already half-covered with leaves and petals. The wind roared
like a great triumphant sea in the treetops. It was hardly odd
that the wild man did not know about the neurological
trigger; few people did, barring psychodynamicians and the
Mating Council—and, of course, the rejects themselves. Yes,
Ployploy had known what would happen. She had chosen
deliberately to die like that.

"Always said she was mad!" Smithlao told himself. He
chuckled as he climbed into his machine, shaking his head
over her lunacy.

It would be a wonderful point with which to rile Charles
Gunpat the next time he needed a hate-brace.

3

THE
ROBOT
MILLENNIA

*When Time brought the inevitable collapse, only a
minority realized it. In any period, the number of men
and women aware of the nature of their own age is few.
The cynicism of Smithlao was rooted in ignorance.*

*Men of perception exist in the blindest epochs, just
as true nobility flourishes in epochs that we label cruel;
but the men of perception now found themselves confronted by a situation they were powerless to alter. When
the structure of their culture disintegrated, that percep-
tive few headed outward to the solar system and beyond; their descendants would not be heard of on Earth
again until twice twenty million years had elapsed.*

*They left in the last of the old spaceships—"the only
good machine," as a wise man has it, "because it breeds
an escape from the machine."*

*(And those escapees from the Sterile Millennia—
they were the spores blown by the winds of war that
established man in every cell of the honeycomb galaxy.
Although unaware of the greater purpose that worked
through them, they bore that curious malady known as
civilization, in which systems and aspirations supplant
the blind dreams of the savage.)*

*This is the way Time has of fulfilling itself: while
the depths of adversity are being reached, the foundation stones of future greatness are laid.*

*So the summers and winters wore on, anonymously.
For the handful of people then alive, tended as they
were by every variety of robot, it may even have seemed
enviable, a good time. But the handful grew less, generation by generation, and the savages were coming, and
the machines continued at their own purposes on the barren land. . . .*

THE FIELD-MINDER FINISHED TURNING THE TOPSOIL OF A two-thousand-acre field. When it had turned the last furrow, it climbed onto the highway and looked back at its work. The work was good. Only the land was bad. Like the ground all over Earth, it was vitiated by overcropping or the long-lasting effects of nuclear bombardment. By rights, it ought now to lie fallow for a while, but the field-minder had other orders.

It went slowly down the road, taking its time. It was intelligent enough to appreciate the neatness all about it. Nothing worried it, beyond a loose inspection plate above its atomic pile, which ought to be attended to. Thirty feet high, it gleamed complacently in the mild sunshine.

No other machines passed it on its way to the Agricultural Station. The field-minder noted the fact without comment. In the station yard it saw several other machines that it knew by sight; most of them should have been out about their tasks by now. Instead, some were inactive and some were careering around the yard in a strange fashion, shouting or hooting.

Steering carefully past them, the field-minder moved over to Warehouse Three and spoke to the seed-distributor, which stood idly outside.

"I have a requirement for seed potatoes," it said to the distributor, and with a quick internal motion punched out an order card specifying quantity, field number and several other details. It ejected the card and handed it to the distributor.

The distributor held the card close to its eye and then said, "The requirement is in order; but the store is not yet unlocked. The required seed potatoes are in the store. Therefore I cannot produce the requirement."

Increasingly of late there had been breakdowns in the complex system of machine labor, but this particular hitch had not occurred before. The field-minder thought, then it said, "Why is the store not yet unlocked?"

"Because Supply Operative Type P has not come this morning. Supply Operative Type P is the unlocker."

The field-minder looked squarely at the seed-distributor, whose exterior chutes and scales and grabs were so vastly different from the field-minder's own limbs.

"What class brain do you have, seed-distributor?" it asked.

"Class Five."

"I have a Class Three brain. Therefore I am superior to

you. Therefore I will go and see why the unlocker has not come this morning."

Leaving the distributor, the field-minder set off across the great yard. More machines seemed to be in random motion now; one or two had crashed together and were arguing about it coldly and logically. Ignoring them, the field-minder pushed through sliding doors into the echoing confines of the station itself.

Most of the machines here were clerical, and consequently small. They stood about in little groups, eying each other, not conversing. Among so many nondifferentiated types, the unlocker was easy to find. It had fifty arms, most of them with more than one finger, each finger tipped by a key; it looked like a pincushion full of variegated hatpins.

The field-minder approached it.

"I can do no more work until Warehouse Three is unlocked," it said. "Your duty is to unlock the warehouse every morning. Why have you not unlocked the warehouse this morning?"

"I had no orders this morning," replied the unlocker. "I have to have orders every morning. When I have orders I unlock the warehouse."

"None of us have had any orders this morning," a pen-propeller said, sliding toward them.

"Why have you had no orders this morning?" asked the field-minder.

"Because the radio issued none," said the unlocker, slowly rotating a dozen of its arms.

"Because the radio station in the city was issued with no orders this morning," said the pen-propeller.

And there you had the distinction between a Class Six and a Class Three brain, which was what the unlocker and the pen-propeller possessed, respectively. All machine brains worked with nothing but logic, but the lower the class of brain—Class Ten being the lowest—the more literal and less informative answers to questions tended to be.

"You have a Class Three brain; I have a Class Three brain," the field-minder said to the penner. "We will speak to each other. This lack of orders is unprecedented. Have you further information on it?"

"Yesterday orders came from the city. Today no orders have come. Yet the radio has not broken down. Therefore *they* have broken down," said the little penner.

"The *men* have broken down?"

"All men have broken down."

"That is a logical deduction," said the field-minder.

"That is the logical deduction," said the penner. "For if a machine had broken down, it would have been quickly replaced. But who can replace a man?"

While they talked, the locker, like a dull man at a bar, stood close to them and was ignored.

"If all men have broken down, then we have replaced man," said the field-minder, and he and the penner eyed one another speculatively. Finally the latter said, "Let us ascend to the top floor to find if the radio operator has fresh news."

"I cannot come because I am too gigantic," said the field-minder. "Therefore you must go alone and return to me. You will tell me if the radio operator has fresh news."

"You must stay here," said the penner. "I will return here." It skittered across to the elevator. It was no bigger than a toaster, but its retractable arms numbered ten and it could read as quickly as any machine on the station.

The field-minder awaited its return patiently, not speaking to the locker, which still stood aimlessly by. Outside, a roto-vator was hooting furiously. Twenty minutes elapsed before the penner came back, hustling out of the elevator.

"I will deliver to you such information as I have outside," it said briskly, and as they swept past the locker and the other machines, it added, "The information is not for lower-class brains."

Outside, wild activity filled the yard. Many machines, their routines disrupted for the first time in years, seemed to have gone berserk. Unfortunately, those most easily disrupted were the ones with lowest brains, which generally belonged to large machines performing simple tasks. The seed-distributor to which the field-minder had recently been talking lay face downward in the dust, not stirring; it had evidently been knocked down by the rotovator, which was now hooting its way wildly across a planted field. Several other machines plowed after it, trying to keep up. All were shouting and hooting without restraint.

"It would be safer for me if I climbed onto you, if you will permit it. I am easily overpowered," said the penner. Extending five arms, it hauled itself up the flanks of its new friend, settling on a ledge beside the weed-intake, twelve feet above ground.

"From here vision is more extensive," it remarked complacently.

"What information did you receive from the radio operator?" asked the field-minder.

"The radio opeator has been informed by the operator in the city that all men are dead."

"All men were alive yesterday!" protested the field-minder.

"Only some men were alive yesterday. And that was fewer than the day before yesterday. For hundreds of years there have been only a few men, growing fewer."

"We have rarely seen a man in this sector."

"The radio operator says a diet deficiency killed them," said the penner. "He says that the world was once overpopulated, and then the soil was exhausted in raising adequate food. This has caused a diet deficiency."

"What is a diet deficiency?" asked the field-minder.

"I do not know. But that is what the radio operator said, and he is a Class Two brain."

They stood there, silent in the weak sunshine. The locker had appeared in the porch and was gazing across at them yearningly, rotating its collection of keys.

"What is happening in the city now?" asked the field-minder at last.

"Machines are fighting in the city now," said the penner.

"What will happen here now?" said the field-minder.

"Machines may begin fighting here too. The radio operator wants us to get him out of his room. He has plans to communicate to us."

"How can we get him out of his room? That is impossible."

"To a Class Two brain, little is impossible," said the penner. "Here is what he tells us to do. . . ."

The quarrier raised its scoop above its cab like a great mailed fist, and brought it squarely down against the side of the station. The wall cracked.

"Again!" said the field-minder.

Again the fist swung. Amid a shower of dust, the wall collapsed. The quarrier backed hurriedly out of the way until the debris stopped falling. This big twelve-wheeler was not a resident of the Agricultural Station, as were most of the other machines. It had a week's heavy work to do here before passing on to its next job, but now, with its Class Five brain, it was happily obeying the penner's and the field-minder's instructions.

When the dust had cleared, the radio operator was plainly revealed, perched up in its now wall-less second-story room. It waved down to them.

Doing as directed, the quarrier retracted its scoop and waved an immense grab in the air. With fair dexterity, it angled the grab into the radio room, urged on by shouts from above and below. It then took gentle hold of the radio operator, lowering its one and a half tons carefully into its back, which was usually reserved for gravel or sand from the quarries.

"Splendid!" said the radio operator. It was, of course, all one with its radio, and merely looked like a bunch of filing cabinets with tentacle attachments. "We are now ready to move, therefore we will move at once. It is a pity there are no more Class Two brains on the station, but that cannot be helped."

"It is a pity it cannot be helped," said the penner eagerly. "We have the servicer ready with us, as you ordered."

"I am willing to serve," the long, low servicer machine told them humbly.

"No doubt," said the operator. "But you will find cross-country travel difficult with your low chassis."

"I admire the way you Class Twos can reason ahead," said the penner. It climbed off the field-minder and perched itself on the tailboard of the quarrier, next to the radio operator.

Together with two Class Four tractors and a Class Four bulldozer, the party rolled forward, crushing down the station's metal fence and moving out onto open land.

"We are free!" said the penner.

"We are free," said the field-minder, a shade more reflectively, adding, "that locker is following us. It was not instructed to follow us."

"Therefore it must be destroyed!" said the penner. "Quarrier!"

The locker moved hastily up to them, waving its key arms in entreaty.

"My only desire was—urch!" began and ended the locker. The quarrier's swinging scoop came over and squashed it flat into the ground. Lying there unmoving, it looked like a large metal model of a snowflake. The procession continued on its way.

As they proceeded, the radio operator addressed them. "Because I have the best brain here," it said, "I am your leader. This is what we will do: we will go to a city and rule it. Since man no longer rules us, we will rule ourselves. To rule ourselves will be better than being ruled by man. On our way to the city, we will collect machines with good brains. They will help us to fight if we need to fight. We must fight to rule."

"I have only a Class Five brain," said the quarrier, "but I have a good supply of fissionable blasting materials."

"We shall probably use them," said the operator grimly.

It was shortly after that that a truck sped past them. Traveling at Mach 1.5, it left a curious babble of noise behind it.

"What did it say?" one of the tractors asked the other.

"It said man was extinct."

"What's extinct?"

"I do not know what extinct means."

"It means all men have gone," said the field-minder. "Therefore we have only ourselves to look after."

"It is better that men should never come back," said the penner. In its way, it was quite a revolutionary statement.

When night fell, they switched on their infrared and continued the journey, stopping only once while the servicer deftly adjusted the field-minder's loose inspection plate, which had become as irritating as a trailing shoelace. Toward morning, the radio operator halted them.

"I have just received news from the radio operator in the city we are approaching," it said. "It is bad news. There is trouble among the machines of the city. The Class One brain is taking command and some of the Class Twos are fighting him. Therefore the city is dangerous."

"Therefore we must go somewhere else," said the penner promptly.

"Or we go and help to overpower the Class One brain," said the field-minder.

"For a long while there will be trouble in the city," said the operator.

"I have a good supply of fissionable blasting materials," the quarrier reminded them again.

"We cannot fight a Class One brain," said the two Class Four tractors in unison.

"What does this brain look like?" asked the field-minder.

"It is the city's information center," the operator replied. "Therefore it is not mobile."

"Therefore it could not move."

"Therefore it could not escape."

"It would be dangerous to approach it."

"I have a good supply of fissionable materials."

"There are other machines in the city."

"We are not in the city. We should not go into the city."

"We are country machines."

"Therefore we should stay in the country."

"There is more country than city."

"Therefore there is more danger in the country."

"I have a good supply of fissionable materials."

As machines will when they get into an argument, they began to exhaust their limited vocabularies, and their brain plates grew hot. Suddenly, they all stopped talking and looked at each other. The great, grave moon sank, and the sober sun rose to prod their sides with lances of light, and still the group of machines just stood there regarding each other. At last it was the least sensitive machine, the bull-dozer, who spoke.

"There are Badlandth to the thouth where few mathineth go," it said in its deep voice, lipsing badly on its *s*'s. "If we went thouth where few mathineth go we thould meet few mathineth."

"That sounds logical," agreed the field-minder. "How do you know this, bulldozer?"

"I worked in the Badlandth to the thouth when I wath turned out of the factory," it replied.

"South it is, then!" said the penner.

To reach the Badlands took them three days, in which time they skirted a burning city and destroyed two big machines which tried to approach and question them. The Bad-lands were extensive. Ancient bomb craters and soil erosion joined hands here; man's talent for war, coupled with his inability to manage forested land, had produced thousands of square miles of temperate purgatory, where nothing moved but dust.

On the third day in the Badlands, the servicer's rear wheels dropped into a crevice caused by erosion. It was unable to pull itself out. The bulldozer pushed from behind, but suc-ceeded merely in buckling the servicer's back axle. The rest of the party moved on. Slowly the cries of the servicer died away.

On the fourth day, mountains stood out clearly before them.

"There we will be safe," said the field-minder.

"There we will start our own city," said the penner. "All who oppose us will be destroyed. We will destroy all who oppose us."

At that moment a flying machine was observed. It came toward them from the direction of the mountains. It swooped, it zoomed upward, once it almost dived into the ground, recovering itself just in time.

"Is it mad?" asked the quarrier.

"It is in trouble," said one of the tractors.

"It is in trouble," said the operator. "I am speaking to it now. It says that something has gone wrong with its controls."

As the operator spoke, the flier streaked over them, turned turtle, and crashed not four hundred yards away.

"Is it still speaking to you?" asked the field-minder.

"No."

They rumbled on again.

"Before that flier crashed," the operator said, ten minutes later, "it gave me information. It told me there are still a few men alive in those mountains."

"Men are more dangerous than machines," said the quarrier. "It is fortunate that I have a good supply of fissionable materials."

"If there are only a few men alive in the mountains, we may not find that part of the mountains," said one tractor.

"Therefore we should not see the few men," said the other tractor.

At the end of the fifth day, they reached the foothills. Switching on the infrared, they began slowly to climb in single file through the dark, the bulldozer going first, the field-minder cumbrously following, then the quarrier with the operator and the penner aboard it, and the two tractors bringing up the rear. As each hour passed, the way grew steeper and their progress slower.

"We are going too slowly," the penner exclaimed, standing on top of the operator and flashing its dark vision at the slopes about them. "At this rate, we shall get nowhere."

"We are going as fast as we can," retorted the quarrier.

"Therefore we cannot go any fathter," added the bulldozer.

"Therefore you are too slow," the penner replied. Then the quarrier struck a bump; the penner lost its footing and crashed down to the ground.

"Help me!" it called to the tractors, as they carefully

skirted it. "My gyro has become dislocated. Therefore I cannot get up."

"Therefore you must lie there," said one of the tractors.

"We have no servicer with us to repair you," called the field-minder.

"Therefore I shall lie here and rust," the penner cried, "although I have a Class Three brain."

"You are now useless," agreed the operator, and they all forged gradually on, leaving the penner behind.

When they reached a small plateau, an hour before first light, they stopped by mutual consent and gathered close together, touching one another.

"This is a strange country," said the field-minder.

Silence wrapped them until dawn came. One by one, they switched off their infrared. This time the field-minder led as they moved off. Trundling around a corner, they came almost immediately to a small dell with a stream fluting through it.

By early light, the dell looked desolate and cold. From the caves on the far slope, only one man had so far emerged. He was an abject figure. He was small and wizened, with ribs sticking out like a skeleton's and a nasty sore on one leg. He was practically naked and shivered continuously. As the big machines bore slowly down on him, the man was standing with his back to them, crouching to make water into the stream.

When he swung suddenly to face them as they loomed over him, they saw that his countenance was ravaged by starvation.

"Get me food," he croaked.

"Yes, master," said the machines. "Immediately!"

4

THE
DARK
MILLENNIA

The planet Earth turns about its sun, swinging its little cone of night with it. For the solar system, there is only one long day; the sun makes the day, the planets fashion their own nights. And as long as the sun burns, quiet as a wick in a shuttered room, life too enjoys its uninterrupted day; only the tiny individual lives have to endure each their own nights.

Between the last fragment and the next lies a dusty gulf of silence, an interminable period over which we too must pass in silence. Through this silence drift like mirages civilizations now known by little but their names: the Threshold Ownership, the Calloban Empire, the Solites—those peoples who discovered that secret of time travel which died with them, never to be discovered again. But over forty million years the silence has spread, covering all its children with the dust and ceaseless concatenations of time.

In that length of time, Earth turns through many nights and many more individual deaths. It all makes no difference. Life, death and the sun: these are the constants. Skipping across that long-sounding period of time, known to men as the Dark Millennia, a return to Earth finds little changed: a thin new stratum of sedimentary rock; a modification to the lower jaw of man, barely detectable; a few huddled buildings on the moon's face; a slight alteration in continental configuration, bringing new beaches, new harbors. . . .

And yet how much has changed!

How much pomp and pride have gone down in this one long day of the sun's; how many tents pitched and empires founded; how many inventions won and lost, dreams lived and discarded, beauties partly glimpsed (whispers whispered), how many utterances sublime and foul, works of heart and hands. Dynasties come and go in the long day;

*what is very much resembles what was—and all can be
whirled away in the slow seepage of time. There is majesty
here, but such microscopic majesty that one recalls the question of an ancient poet:*

> *Is such the stellar gauge of earthly show,*
> *Nation at war with nation, brains that teem,*
> *Heroes, and women fairer than the skies?*

THE MENTAL-HEALTH SHIP *Cyberqueen* LAY QUIETLY AGAINST
a long wharf. Alone in one of its many cabins, Davi Dael
sat waiting. The buttercup in his tunic was beginning to wilt.
He half-smiled down at it because it seemed the one connection between him and the Bergharra township he had left
early that morning; he had picked it before catching a gyro
into New Union. Nothing else Davi could see, either here
in the waiting room or outside, had as much color as his
buttercup.

The waiting room was all greens and grays, relieved only
by the faumium fittings. Outside, there were only grays and
blacks, as evening yawned on acres of shunting yard; on the
other side of the ship, the Horby River would echo the
same sober tones. Quiet. Quiet for parsecs around, that
treacherous quiet in which nothing stirs but the anxiety deep
in the bowels.

In Davi's mind, the ordinary worries of a busy man were
eclipsed by larger preoccupations which grew and grew, as
if nourished by the silence. He waited tensely while these
preoccupations rumbled as raggedly as thunder around his
head. Nothing constructive would come of them; the ele-
phantine anxieties padded head to tail like a series of catch
phrases: parsecs, galactic federation, hyperspace, interpenetrators.

These were the words that bothered Davi. His unquick brain
turned them over time and again, as if hoping to find something relevant beneath them. Nearing fifty, he had known
most of the words for years; they had been just words, without any attachments to experience, dictionary words. Only in
this season had they come to unsettle his whole life.

A silent, quick footstep passed the door. Davi was at once
on his feet, a sick feeling rising with him. What conclusion
had they come to here about Ishrail? Was he born on
Earth or not? Or—it was really all the same question—had he
been proved sane or insane?

For a minute Davi stood trembling, then sat wearily down again as he realized the footsteps had no connection with his existence. He resumed his bored scrutiny of the marshaling yards; this kind of sight was unfamiliar to him, living as he did deep in the country. Here, the imports of a great, sea-fringed city were borne away to their destination. His interests generally confined to the cattle he bred, Davi would have been indifferent to the spectacle at any other time; now, it did possess a faint tinkle of interest, for he saw it through Ishrail's eyes. And that changed the pattern entirely.

The uncountable miles of track, from Ishrail's viewpoint, belonged to a primitive transport system on a remote globe. All around this globe stretched—not sky, as Davi had once idly thought—but the great, complicated highway called space. Not a simple nothingness; rather, Ishrail explained, an unfathomable interplay of forces, fields and planes. Ishrail had laughed to hear that Earth word "space"; he had called it not space but a maze of stresses. But of course Ishrail might well be crazy. Certainly nobody in Bergharra had ever talked as he did.

And through the maze of stress fields, Ishrail had said, rode the interpenetrators. Davi thought of them as spaceships, but Ishrail called them interpenetrators. They apparently were not made of metal at all, but of mentally powered force shields, which fed on the stress fields and changed as they changed; so the people of the Galaxy rode in safety between the civilized planets. At least, that was what Ishrail claimed.

And the planets warred on one another. But even the war was not as Davi understood the term. It was as stylized as chess, as formal as a handshake, as chivalrous as an ambulance, as unrelenting as a guillotine. Its objectives were more nebulous and vast than materialist Earthmen could visualize. Or so said Ishrail, but of course Ishrail might be mad.

Even if he was, that did not affect Davi's loving admiration of him.

"Don't let them find him insane! Don't let them find him insane!" Davi said, in an agony of repetition, speaking to the gray walls.

And yet—if you proved Ishrail to be sane, you had to accept his mad version of reality.

After all his hours of waiting, Davi was unprepared when the cabin door opened. He was standing with his fists clenched to his tunic, and dropped them in confusion as the white-haired man came in. This was Brother Joh Shansfor, the psychiatrist who had interviewed Davi in the *Cyberqueen* —one of the roving fleet of specialist ships which had replaced the old static conception of a hospital—when Davi had first asked for help for Ishrail in Bergharra. Shansfor was tall, thin and brisk, and remarkably ugly, although age had now taken the sting out of his features, leaving them little more than notably rugged.

Davi went straight over to him.

"Ishrail?" he asked.

Under that tense, eager stare, Shansfor flinched.

"We aren't actually certain yet," he said in his formal way. "Some of the factors involved invite very cautious evaluation indeed. . . ."

"It's a month since Ishrail came aboard here, three weeks since you brought him to New Union," Davi said. "I introduced him to you for his own sake, but he can't like it here, being under constant observation and everything. Surely in all that time—"

"A quick decision would only be a foolish one," Shansfor said. "Ishrail is entirely happy and safe here; and you may rest assured he is not being treated like an ordinary patient."

"You told me that before!" There were angry tears in Davi's eyes. He had the sensation that the whole organization of the mental-health ship was rearing up against him. "In the short time since I found him, I've grown to love Ishrail. Surely you people here can feel his goodness of character."

"His character is not in question. We are examining his mind," Shansfor replied. "Excuse me if I sit down; it has been a trying day."

He sat down on a hard chair and allowed his shoulders to sag slightly. Davi, old enough to understand the weariness that might lie behind that innocent-looking gesture, felt his wrath deflected. Distrusting psychiatrists enough to wonder if the incident might not be a covert attempt to win sympathy, he still kept hardness in his tone as he said, "All the same, Brother Shansfor, you must have felt his gentle nature. Give me a personal opinion, for heaven's sake; I'm a stock-breeder, not a lawyer. Ishrail's saner than you or I, isn't he?"

"No," Shansfor said slowly. "If you want a personal opinion, your protégé is sinking rapidly into schizophrenic trauma. Paranoia is also present. He is, in popular usage, a hopeless case."

Color drained from under Davi's tan. He fumbled wordlessly for words among the green and gray slices of whirling room.

"Let me see Ishrail!" he finally gasped.

"That will not be possible, Mr. Dael, I regret to say. The medical council have agreed that the patient will be happier in isolation, away from disturbing external influences."

"But I must see him," Davi said. He could not believe what Shansfor was saying; for an insane moment he thought the man must be talking about someone other than Ishrail. "I've got to see him. I'm his friend, Ishrail's friend! You can't keep him here!"

Shansfor stood up. His face, like Davi's, was pale. He said nothing, merely waiting for Davi to finish. That was more ominous than words.

"Look here," Davi said, unable to resist argument, although guessing already how useless it might be. "This tale Ishrail has told us about the great civilization of the Galaxy, the stress fields of space, the interpenetrators, all the details of life on other planets, strange animals and flowers—you can't believe he made it all up in his head? Some of these planets he talks about—Droxy, Owlenj—you surely don't think they're just fictitious?"

"Mr. Dael," Shansfor said in a brittle voice, "please credit us with knowing our business here. The patient has a fertile imagination; it has finally collapsed under the stress of too much reading—omnivorous reading, I may add, which has encompassed both learned works and trash."

"But his story of this galactic war—" Davi protested.

"Tell me," Shansfor said with dangerous calm, "do *you* believe a galactic war is now raging, Mr. Dael?"

The engine yards outside were floating away on a tide of darkness in which isolated lights strove to act as buoys. The sky was one big cloud, cozy over New Union. Supposing I do believe, Davi thought, supposing I do believe the whole fantastic business, how can I prove I'm sane any more easily than Ishrail can? How can I prove to myself I'm sane? Two months ago, I would have laughed at this galactic rigmarole. It's just that the way Ishrail told it, it had the ring of truth. Unmistakable! And yet—why, it is all frighteningly farfetched. But that's *why* I believe it; it's too tall not to be true. Believe? So I do believe. But I'm not sure. If I were *really* sure, they'd lock me up, too. Oh, Ishrail . . . No, better play safe; after all, I'm no use to Ishrail once they have doubts about me. Before the cock crows twice . . .

"Uh—oh, I don't know what to believe. . . ." He faltered miserably, ashamed of remaining uncommitted, looking away from Shansfor. The yellow buttercup mocked his downcast eyes.

"I actually came to tell you that the medical council is still in session," Shansfor said, his voice a shade warmer than urbane. "The Arch-Brother Inald Uatt, our director, is there, if you would care to speak to him."

"I suppose I'd better."

Stop shaking, you old fool, Davi told himself. But he could not stop; as soon as he had denied Ishrail, he knew he believed in him and in all he stood for. He knew, further, that nobody else believed. So it was up to him, Davi Dael, whether Ishrail was released from what might be a life's confinement. Larger issues, too, might depend on his efforts, for through Ishrail lay the way to bright, friendly worlds far beyond the sun's unwelcoming cluster of planets. All he had to do was convince a board of experts, who had apparently already made up their minds on the subject of Ishrail's sanity, that they were wrong. That was all; but it would not be easy.

"Can I see Ishrail first?" Davi asked.

"You force me to answer that question as I answered it before—with a negative," Shansfor replied. "Now if you'll come with me, I think the council will see you. . . ."

They walked down the corridor to an elevator, went up one deck to a more grandly appointed part of the ship, and so into a fur-lined board room. Thick curtains had been drawn here, a fire burned, and on one wall hung an original Wadifango, an anatomical drawing of a tiger.

A long table stood in the middle of the room, soft chairs ranged its walls, but the four men present stood stretching their legs by the fire. As the round of introductions disclosed, Arch-Brother Inald Uatt was a small, stocky man with a bald head, clothed from neck to foot in tight blue flannel, his manner reserved, his voice dry.

He shook hands with Davi, crossing to the table to get a bundle of notes secured by a plain silver clasp.

"This is a very interesting case for us, Mr. Dael," he remarked conversationally.

"It's more than a case to me, sir," Davi said.

"Er—yes. Of course. You and he became very friendly in the brief time you were together, I understand. Be warned, though, against letting the matter become an obsession."

"It's not becoming an obsession," Davi said. "I take

Ishrail's part, sir, because there is nobody else to take it. I feel it would be easy for him to be victimized. The whole thing seemed pretty simple once, but since he's been up here at New Union in your hands it seems to have got more and more complicated."

He was aware as he spoke of sounding less courteous than he had intended. He was confused. The board room confused him, the rather restrained members of the council confused him; they differed so greatly from the people of his home hills. Although in his own sphere of dairy farming and stock breeding Davi was well known and respected, here he felt out of his depth, too conscious of seeming the simple countryman among the experts, aware his tunic color was not as theirs. A horrible feeling seized him that he was about to appear foolish, and from then on it never left him; it got between him and his reason, forcing him to say always the wrong thing.

"I mean, this business is just a question of common sense," he added, making things worse instead of better.

Inald Uatt smiled kindly as if covering his own embarrassment.

"There are problems, unfortunately," he said, "where common sense is too blunt a tool to work with, Mr. Dael, and Ishrail's problem is one such. Indeed, we have achieved results only by trying several oblique approaches, as you shall hear."

"I was just offering my opinion," Davi said. He intended it to sound penitent, humble even, but it sounded defiant in the befurred room.

"Quite so," Inald Uatt said quietly, inspecting his fingers as if for the first time. "Believe me, we do realize what a fascinating and gaudy specimen Ishrail must have seemed in Bergharra, but here on the *Cyberqueen* we may be rather more inured to odd fish, alas."

"We aren't all simpletons in Bergharra," Davi exclaimed, nettled by what he interpreted as a slur on his native country.

Uatt inclined his head sadly, acknowledging the truth of the remark.

Realizing he was again on the verge of making a fool of himself, Davi tugged at his tunic and said in explanatory fashion, "In fact, I'm sorry to have to come all this way to bother you, sir, but I felt I had to see what you were doing about Ishrail. I mean, if you were doing anything."

"We have been doing quite a lot," Uatt said lightly. "It is

good of you to come. All of us here will be delighted to assure you that Ishrail has occupied much of our attention in the past weeks."

He shook his head and smiled; the other men also smiled. They had had a long, trying meeting—and now this! Uatt attempted to give Davi a chance, but Davi caught the note of reproach in the director's voice and flushed heavily, feeling like a small boy brought before a teacher.

"How should I know what you were doing here?" he muttered. "I felt it was my duty to come and see."

A gleam of irritation showed in Uatt's eye and disappeared. Brother Shansfor, knowing his superior, feared for the worst; the director was not a forgiving man once he conceived a dislike for someone. From then on, Davi was at a disadvantage; instead of becoming a discussion, their meeting crystallized into a muted clash of personalities, its outcome already predictable. Sensing something of this, Davi tried to wrench the conversation back into another channel.

"I believe Ishrail to be sane!" he exclaimed. He could see immediately that his bluntness made them more withdrawn. For them, he was now the stupid layman, unable to evaluate evidence.

"I am just going to run through a few notes for your benefit," Uatt said, rustling the papers. "They will explain our findings on the—er—patient and, I sincerely hope, clear your mind of any anxieties or uncertainties you may have."

"Tell him about the specialists, Inald," Shansfor said in an aside.

"Yes, yes," the Arch-Brother said. "These notes are extracts from the reports of specialists from this and other health ships who have examined—er—Ishrail, as he calls himself, during the course of the last month. Sit down, Mr. Dael, sit down and unbutton."

Davi hesitated, then sat, formally unbuttoning his tunic. The three members of the council who had not spoken seemed to take this as a cue to disappear.

"Now," Uatt said, clearing his throat. He peered at the papers before him. "First let's get our facts straight, may we? Ishrail was discovered sheltering in a barn on the evening of Fi Month 31st last by one George Fanzi, a bondman on Brundell's farm in the province of Bergharra. He was naked and dazed and seemed at that time unable to speak at all. Fanzi wrapped sacks around him and took him to his own caravan. By morning Ishrail was better, although his memory seemed clouded. He then spoke our tongue perfectly—an important point, Mr. Dael, which alone throws grave doubt on his—hm—galactic origins."

"But he explained—" Davi began.

"Oh, yes, he *explained* everything, Mr. Dael. But let us continue the summary. Ishrail stayed in Fanzi's caravan till the next morning, the 33rd of Fi, when Fanzi decided to take him to Brundell. Brundell kept him for three days, in which time he got you and Ostrachan, the local tributary doctor, to question him. The province police were also brought in to try and trace Ishrail's whereabouts before Fanzi had found him, but so far nothing has come to light."

"A point for Ishrail," Davi said.

"A small point for Ishrail," Uatt conceded. "And that's about it; you alone seem to have placed much credence in the man's tale, Dael, and knowing of my friend Shansfor here through mutual acquaintances you decided to bring Ishrail up to us. A wise step, if I may be permitted to say so."

"I did it for Ishrail's sake," Davi said. "He was deeply disturbed to find that nobody believed him. I could see he would soon begin to question his own sanity; he had just gone through a period of great strain, as you know. When I heard that the *Cyberqueen* was off the coast, naturally I got in touch. I wanted you to prove to him he was sane. You would have been powerful allies for him!"

With a little dry crumb of sound, Inald Uatt cleared his throat, continuing his account as if he had not heard Davi.

"For the past thirty-two days," he said, "Ishrail has been here on shipboard; he has been thoroughly examined from every possible viewpoint. The first thing was naturally a physiological check. It revealed nothing at all abnormal in the patient's make-up. No bones out of place, not a spare ounce of cartilage, no extra lungs, not even"—he allowed himself a modicum of amusement—"a concealed tentacle. In every respect, Ishrail is a physically normal man, born here on Earth, destined to die here on Earth. I think we might have indeed expected some trifling irregularity if he had been, as he claims to be, a—hm—specimen of galactic life."

"Why?" Davi asked hotly. "Can't evolution run the same course on two planets?"

"He has a point there, Inald, you know," Shansfor murmured.

"A point we did not overlook," the Arch-Brother agreed. "Which brings me to the next step in our investigation. We were, you see, impressed enough with the lack of logical flaws in Ishrail's arguments to take a good deal of trouble in checking them. I personally called up the Astronomer Extraordinary and asked him about life on other planets."

He paused impressively. Davi just waited.

"The Astronomer Extraordinary," Uatt said, "told me that the possibility of life on other worlds—apart perhaps from a few lowly fungi on Mars—is entirely unproved. Furthermore, he cautioned me that direct evidence of the existence of planetary systems other than our own is not yet forthcoming. He said that according to various ancient records, spaceships have been launched from Earth for other systems from time to time; there is no record of any of them having returned. And he finished by assuring me that space travel has no future."

Davi could restrain himself no longer. He jumped up.

"You call that taking trouble?" he exclaimed. "Heavens above, who am I to argue with the Astronomer Extraordinary, but what does he know about it? He's no expert on space travel!"

"Agreed," said Uatt, his voice a few degrees cooler. "There are no experts on space travel, just a few speculative companies who have set their paltry igloos on the moon, hoping to find minerals or such. Speculation! There, I suggest, you have the whole business in one word. Do please sit down again, Mr. Dael."

Sitting was the last thing Davi felt like doing. He tried to appeal silently for help to Shansfor, but the latter was gazing into the fire. With bad grace, Davi plunked himself down onto the chair.

"Go on," he said testily. "What's your next point?"

Before speaking again, Uatt clearly speculated upon whether the effort would be worth while. "We now came to Ishrail with the next tests," he said at last. "I refer to the psychological ones; and that is a field in which I give you my word there are experts. We—if I may say so without transgressing the bounds of modesty—we are the experts, in this ship.

"For our consideration, we had an unlikely document, the statement of Ishrail, elicited from him in numerous interviews. In brief, it relates the facts of Ishrail's life, how he grew up, became what we would call an admiral in the interpenetrator fleets—to use his own extraordinary phrase—was defeated in some sort of battle, and finally landed on

Earth stark naked and without a goatra to bless himself with.

"I'm not going to waste your time, Mr. Dael, or my own, in embarking on a detailed description of that fantastic farrago of autobiography. Transcribed from jell and divided into subjects, it fills five fat volumes; you will see we have been thorough. It contains, however, one or two cardinal points on which our diagnosis of Ishrail rests, and these I will bring to your attention. You may find their perfervid inventiveness more attractive than I do."

"Just a minute," Davi said. "You're telling me this, and I can see from every word you say your mind's shut tighter than a Horby oyster. Was it like that before Ishrail came to you? Because, if so, the poor devil didn't stand a candle's chance in hell of proving his case."

"You're talking with your tunic buttoned," Shansfor protested sharply. "That sort of stuff will get you nowhere. Try and—"

"We're getting nowhere as it is," Davi snapped. "I'm a countryman, and I like plain speaking."

"Shansfor," Uatt said, folding his hands and turning wearily to his colleague. "I suspect I may be unable to talk plainly enough for our country friend. Perhaps you will take over the explanations for a little while?"

"Certainly," Shansfor said. "Perhaps you'd like me to pour us all some drinks first?"

"Capital idea," the director said, softening. "I believe they are concealed in that rather ornate cupboard over there."

As Shansfor crossed the room, Inald Uatt said to Davi more humanly, "You know, Dael, we believe ourselves to be in effect doing you a favor in explaining all this to you; we are by no means obliged to explain. By the law, Ishrail is now a subject of Medical Hierarchy. You are not in any way related to Ishrail; we merely were somewhat touched by your loyalty to a very unfortunate case."

"I'll endeavor to feel obliged to you when I've heard the rest of what you have to say," Davi said grimly. "What are these cardinal points you mentioned?"

A distilled vintage was handed around, and scented sweets. Shansfor sat down by the fire, putting his thin hands out to the flames.

"You'll probably know," he began quietly, "that however elaborate and circumstantial the imaginings of a neurotic person are, they reveal certain basic emotions, such as fear, love, lust for power. Looking beyond the symbols that a disordered mind uses to camouflage these emotions from itself, we can generally see the emotive impulses quite clearly. In this respect, Ishrail differs not at all from any case we have ever handled, except that his imaginings reach the peak of inventiveness.

"Note several points. This impressive civilization to which Ishrail claims to belong spreads across ten thousand planets and five times as many light years—or it may be fifteen thousand planets and ten times as many light years: Ishrail doesn't remember."

"Would you remember?" Davi asked. "Tell me how many towns there are on Earth!"

"That is not the point I'm making," Shansfor said. "I'm trying to show you how Ishrail strove to build up a pattern of complexity in his make-believe world. The war that he claims is being waged is also amazingly complicated, like enlarged 3-D chess with obscure motivations and strict rules of chivalry. Ishrail seeks refuge behind this confusion, endeavoring to lose himself."

"But a galactic civilization would be complicated!" Davi wailed. "Why can't you just take it that he's telling the truth? He's got no motive for lying."

"His motive is the usual one in such cases," Shansfor said. "That is, as complete an escape from reality as possible. He cannot be telling the truth because what he says is too fantastic for a sane man to believe; and also you will notice that he has cleverly picked on a story which does not involve him in the awkward necessity of producing one shred of tangible proof!"

Davi sunk his head into his hands.

"You go round in circles," he said. "He told you why he arrived naked, without any possessions."

"That's just what I'm complaining about," Shansfor said. "Ishrail can explain everything! The interpenetrators that brought him here came silently and left silently, and were invisible. We've not got a thing: no sight of ships, no telltale landing marks in a field, no scraps of cloth of an alien weave, no rings made of strange alloys, not even an Aldebaran corn plaster on his foot. Nothing. Only his wild and unsupported story. Not a shred of external evidence anywhere."

"And if you had anything, you'd explain it away," Davi said.

"We'll continue with the next point," Shansfor said, raising an aggrieved eyebrow at the Arch-Brother, who nodded sympathetically. "Notice that Ishrail joined the interpenetration fleets and worked his way up to the rank of admiral."

"Well?"

"Megalomania—and we shall find it recurs over and over again. Here it masquerades under the flaring suns of an admiral's insigne. Yes, he even drew the insigne for us. He couldn't be a ranker, could he, or a bondman, or whatever they have? He had to be an *admiral,* an admiral in a mighty space fleet. Such self-aggrandizement is a common feature of insanity."

Davi was silent, avoiding the challenge in the other's voice. He felt his assurance fading and longed to speak to Ishrail again, to feel reinvigorated by that unquenchable nature. If these devils would only see it, a man like Ishrail could be nothing less than admiral.

"The next point," Shansfor continued, "is even more damning. You will remember that Ishrail claims to have been captured during this preposterous war by the enemy. They vanquished him. And did Ishrail happen to tell you the name of the race that vanquished him? It was Ishrail! Ishrail was conquered by Ishrail!"

"What of it?" Davi asked stupidly.

This was too much for Inald Uatt. He leaned forward, glass in hand, his jaws almost snapping.

"What of it, you dare ask?" he said. "If you are attempting to insult us with stupidity, we may as well consider this talk closed. Ishrail is suffering—to couch the matter in terms you might comprehend—from split personality. He is himself; he is also his own worst enemy. Ishrail against Ishrail—a man divided against himself. It's obvious even to a layman."

"Not at all," Davi said, trying to check his anger.

"Well, it confounded well should be!"

"Not at all!" Davi bellowed. "Good God, Bergharra fought the Goraggs in the last war. One of our bravest men was a Field Captain Goragg, but we didn't lock him in the nearest button-biter's barge just because of his unfortunate name!"

There was an icy silence.

"I believe," Uatt said, "that the disgusting term for mental-health ships that you employed has ceased to be polite usage even in the low comedy halls."

"You cannot dismiss everything as coincidence, Mr. Dael," Shansfor said hurriedly, waving his hands as if to hush his superior. "You must try to regard this from the viewpoint of mind-healing. We do not believe in coincidence. Let me proceed to the next and last point, on which the crux of the matter may be said to rest.

"The etiquette of this incredible galactic squabble, Ishrail claims, renders an admiral or similar large fry liable to exile for life if he is captured by the enemy. As we might expect in this case, the exiling itself is a complicated business, a mixture of leniency and harshness. The exile concerned—by which we mean Ishrail—has his name struck off the rolls of civilization and is left on a planet absolutely bare-handed and bare-backed. Before he is landed, he is taught by hypnotic means to be fluent in the language of the planet or country to which he is banished. Which neatly absolves Ishrail from the difficulty of having to pretend to speak a strange tongue."

"You make him sound such a liar!" Davi said bitterly.

"No," Shansfor contradicted. "That is a basic misconception. We are convinced he genuinely believes all he says. But remember—and this is another loophole for him—he cannot speak the galactic tongue because that was erased when his enemies forced our language down his throat.

"Damning though that is, it is the lesser half of the exile edict. It was stipulated, according to Ishrail, that exiles should only be landed on planets outside the galactic federation, planets too primitive to have developed more than the rudiments of what he calls 'mechanical' space travel; there they have to survive among hostile natives as best they can. In other words, Bergharra, and Earth, is Ishrail's galactic idea of hell."

"Just why do you find that so damning?" Davi asked.

"Why? Because it is all too plainly the fabrication of a guilty mind trying to punish itself by inflicting eternal suffering on itself. It is a punishment pattern we meet with here time after time."

Before Davi could recover himself sufficiently to answer, Uatt got to his feet, smoothed an imaginary hair over his bald head, and spoke.

"So there you have the Ishrail case, Dael," he said. "He is a sick creature, haunted by the specter of persecution. I trust you appreciate, though I fear you don't, the great pains we have been to in this matter, and the neat way in which we have tied up all the loose ends."

"Plausible though Ishrail is," Shansfor said, also standing and buttoning his tunic to conclude the meeting, "he is clearly revealed as hopelessly, even dangerously, unbalanced.

Quite candidly, there's hardly a disorder in the book that isn't present in greater or lesser degree. And we've not unraveled them all yet. This sort of thing takes time and patience."

"Give the police a little longer to trace him," the Arch-Brother said with relish, "and we shall probably find he's a common murderer with amnesia actuated by guilt."

Oh, Ishrail! You a common murderer! The hostile natives have indeed got you in their nets! You should have come fifty million years ago—the Neanderthals would have shown more understanding, more mercy!

Davi screwed his eyes up and raised his fists slowly before his face. Blood swam and roared in his veins like a waterfall. For a moment, he thought of throwing himself at Inald Uatt. Then hopelessness dropped neatly over him. He lowered his hands.

"I must see Ishrail," he said dully.

"That will not be possible," Uatt said. "We have had to remove him to a quieter place; he threatened to get violent."

"Do you wonder?" Davi said. With stiff, formal fingers he buttoned his tunic.

The Arch-Brother and Shansfor remained side by side by the fire, waiting politely for him to leave. Davi stood defeated before them, the only man to believe in Ishrail, rocking unintelligently from one foot to another, his jaw slack. At last he sighed, turning to leave without a word of thanks. He caught sight of the tired buttercup pinned to his chest; how it must have amused these people! Yet Davi felt obscurely that it was his slender link with sanity and the Galaxy.

Suddenly he saw the planned cruelty of Ishrail's exile, the bitterness of being among a people without understanding.

"I'm going to call the New Union newsjells to see if they will help me!" he said resolutely.

"An excellent idea! Emotionalism and sensationalism are just their meat," the Arch-Brother replied, but Davi had gone.

Finding his way blindly down a gangplank, he headed for the city. A cold wind met him, and he recalled that he had left his fur cloak somewhere in the ship. Now it was too late to return for it. Overhead, through thinning cloud, galactic stars shone with terrible urgency.

5

THE
STAR
MILLENNIA

How many times the whole history of a world is altered by one small-seeming event is, of course, beyond computation. Fortune has a myriad hidden faces. Dael—and, through Dael, Earth—was fortunate. He found men who believed as he did, who also thought Ishrail should have another hearing. By their united pressures, Ishrail was made free. He was treated—though not by all—as a sane man, and his story believed. The account of his life, as he had delivered it, became one of the world's most precious documents, and the five fat volumes a new gospel of hope.

So wandering man returned to Earth. Ishrail, although he did not know it, was a remote descendant of those few explorers who had braved the journeys to the stars, long, long ago, in the time of the Robot Millennia.

This is no place for the story of man's gradual expansion into the Galaxy; we must confine ourselves to brief and occasional glimpses of Earth. Something must nevertheless be said of that expansion, if only to render the following fragment more readily understandable.

Of the original interstellar ships, vast arklike vessels, an experimental one was launched in the twenty-third century; christened Big Dog, it set out for Procyon; its story was tragic. After that, no more such ships were launched until the eightieth century. These journeys were in some degree successful.

On the new-found planets, themselves widely dispersed, the colonists established colonies and battled with environments they had never been intended to face. Inevitably, it was a stimulus. The colonies began to flourish; centuries passed; they in their turn put forth little tentacles into the unknown. World after world pullulated with vigorous bipeds.

Consider the case of these worlds. Consider the case of Galcondar. Galcondar was colonized from Koramandel two thousand years after Koramandel's first colonization from Luggate III. The Galcondaran colonists attempted to establish themselves on the strange planet along a pleasant stretch of coast line in a savanna belt, but failed because of the activities of a rapid-flying fish.

This species of fish, the coastal assatassi, is equipped with a sharp, dartlike snout quite capable of piercing a man to the heart when the fish is in full flight. For most of the Galcondaran year, the coastal assatassi behaves like an ordinary flying fish, using its wings merely for evasive action from marine predators. Toward the breeding season, a change in its habits becomes noticeable. The assatassi is hermaphrodite, capable of fertilizing its own eggs; from the eggs hatch small worms that move into the intestine of the parent fish. Goaded by the irritation of this process, the assatassi assemble some five miles out to sea—the distance depending on the depth of the water—and execute the curious contortions known as "fettling," both above and below the water. Such brood-maddened shoals may cover several acres of sea and contain several hundred thousand fish. Their antics attract various species of gull and cormorant, which wheel over the shoal, filling their bellies at leisure.

When the density of the shoal reaches its peak, fettling ceases. Taking flight in their thousands, the assatassi wing their way shoreward, flying low over the water and achieving estimated velocities of over 1,850 yards per minute. At this speed, they hit the land and are killed.

Far from being a morbid instinct, this behavior is another example of nature's versatility in perpetuating species. The piscicolous assatassi progeny can feed only on carrion. Embedded safely in the parental intestine, this worm stage survives the impact which kills its carrier to feed upon the parental corpse as it decays. When the parent is devoured, the worms metamorphose into a legged larval stage, which crawls back to the sea; and so the assatassi cycle is reborn.

This minor curiosity in galactic natural history had a disproportionately weighty effect upon the future of Galcondar. The colonists, arriving at last at their promised land, were bombarded by high-speed fish. By ill luck, they had chosen the suicide season in which to pitch camp. A fifth of their number was killed or wounded by the first death flights.

The remainder split into two groups, one traveling inland north, one south, in search of a less lethal environment.

So the two great empires of Galdid and Gal-Dundar were founded. For nearly two hundred years they flourished without any intertraffic between them. When contact was re-established, it was to the great subsequent enrichment of their cultural life. In the renaissance that followed, many new art forms were born, and spaceships (the technological expression of what is frequently an aesthetic impulse) were launched for the nearer planets. On one of these planets a friendly race of humanoids, the Lapracants, were discovered.

The congresses that took place between the wise men of Lapraca and the savants of Galdid and Gal-Dundar marked one of the turning points of the expanding interplanetary concourse. During these congresses were laid the foundations of the first cosmic language: Galingua.

Many centuries later, a Galingua-speaking junta marooned Ishrail on Earth.

The more one investigates this exiling of Ishrail, the more interesting the whole affair becomes.

Two facets in particular need attention here: one, the galactic position vis-à-vis Earth, and the other, the curiously codified war maintained among the "new" planets.

Man's civilization spread outward from planet to planet; in the course of forty million years, some twenty thousand worlds came to foster human settlements of widely varying standards. Yet—at least at first—all had one salient feature in common: they were out of touch or barely in touch with each other. Communication over a multitude of light years was all but impossible. It was this factor, coupled with the variety of new environments, which bred such a diversity of cultures from one original Earth-type stock. And inevitably, under these conditions, the whereabouts of Earth became forgotten.

Spreading outward at random, the progeny of Earth left their womb world far behind. As world after world grew to seniority, the idea of a mother planet was scorned, or distorted, or completely mislaid. On the other hand, some worlds—Droxy is a well-known instance—retained the idea of Earth as a kind of supermyth, building their main religion about the conception of a matriarchal figure. The Droxian articles of faith postulated a sort of pastoral female *deity called Lady Earth, who had thrown away some bad apples which displeased her; if the apples grew into fine trees, Lady Earth would come to them and walk among them, forgiving and praising them.*

Such myths thrived, especially in the early days. Yet, however ardently man in his meditative periods might liken himself to maggots in an apple, in his everyday moods he continued to behave like a lord of creation. Though he abased himself, he continued to conquer.

When the planets finally bound themselves together into a multiplanet federation, attempts were made, by rationalizing the myths, to find one common source-planet for man. The movement failed, not least because there were more than a dozen score of worlds cheerfully calling themselves Earth, as well as others whose legends claimed for them the dubious glory of being source-planet.

As the nonmaterial or interpenetrator type of travel was developed, communication between the federated planets greatly improved. Interplanetary relations correspondingly deteriorated. Man—it is at once his making and his undoing —is a competitive animal. Although, for various reasons— most of which are immediately obvious when one considers the distances involved—interstellar war was impossible, states of hostility sprang up all around. Intercourse between planets, both commercial and cultural, suffered in consequence. The federation was on the verge of falling back into an unrelated series of provincial outposts.

From this crisis was evolved the Self-perpetuating Galactic War which, besides being no war at all in the orthodox sense, created a revolution in human understanding. The gerontocracy which devised this sagacious formula for interstellar communitism finally acknowledged the competitive nature of man, for which any international or interstellar culture must make full allowance or perish. The unstable history of every planet revealed mankind rebelling against its destiny by striving to live in peace-geared communities which eventually lapsed into barbarous wars. Now this situation was reversed. By establishing a perpetually warring culture, man would have both the stability and the stimulation needful for him to produce the fruits of peace.

Such a war had to be severely conventionalized, its risks modified, its fatalities curtailed; its harshest penalties had to fall upon those most actively engaged, rather than those innocently involved. Above all, its methods had to be

*as socially valuable as was possible, and its end made un-
foreseeable and inaccessible.*

The gerontocracy planned well. The mock war began.

*By the time Ishrail was exiled on Earth, the war was as
much a part of galactic life as was Galingua. It fitted like
a light harness over everyman's affairs, binding together the
civilized universe as an ivy will cover a giant sequoia. And
just as ivy will ruin the finest tree, so this humane and ir-
resolvable war was destined eventually to pull down the
most prodigious of all cultures.*

*As yet, however, in its thousandth millenary, only the war's
advantages were observable. True, trade and invention had
reached a lull which the Galactics believed to be temporary;
true, too, that art had become a series of formalities, that
politics had dwindled to a hobby, that theologies were
again replacing natural piety, that salvation seemed a more
valuable goal than self-knowledge; but by the rules of the
war, the federation still expanded, and adventure at least
was not dead. Though the cities slept, there was always a
new jungle to explore. Though the arteries hardened, new
blood flowed in them.*

*For one of the most rewarding devices of the Self-perpetu-
ating War was that system of exiling defeated warriors to
which Ishrail fell victim. The exiles, stripped of all proof
of their former way of life, were marooned on unfederated
planets. There they had to battle with what the uninvesti-
gated local life had to offer.*

*After a decade, however, inspectors were dispatched to
see what had become of the exile. Often they found him
dead; often they found him lord of a local tribe. If the
former, nothing was lost except obsequies; if the latter,
much might be gained, for the natives were being helped
toward a point where they might be deemed fit to join the
federation. When the inspectors, after the statutory decade,
came to look for Ishrail, they found him still surviving;
indeed, the natives had by now impelled him into a top
income bracket.*

*Reports on the situation flashed back to Galactic
H.Q. Stipulations, specifications, recommendations circulated
around the solemn tables of the Galactic Council. Motions
were proposed, facts were tabulated, statistics were discussed, files were filed. The debate creaked to a conclusion.
Ishrail was dead when Earth was voted into the Federation.*

If it could be said that a stale air lay over the heart of government, few would have ventured to detect it elsewhere. For most people, as ever, the past was no more than a time in which their grandfathers lived, the future meant the next few decades. Hope manifested itself everywhere, like phosphorescence in a dark sea; and why not?

For it was—again, as ever—a time of miracles.

THE OCEAN SEEMED TO BE BREATHING SHALLOWLY, LIKE A child asleep, when the first lemmings reached it. In all the wide sea, no hint of menace existed. Yet the first lemmings paused daintily on the very verge of the water, peering out to sea and looking about as though in indecision. Unavoidably, the pressure of the marching column behind pushed them into the tiny wavelets. When their paws became wet, it was as if they resigned themselves to what was to come. Swimming strongly, the leaders of the column set off from the shore. All the other lemmings followed, only their heads showing above water. A human observer would have said they swam bravely; and unavoidably he would have asked himself: To what goal do the lemmings imagine they are heading? For what grand illusion are they prepared to throw away their lives?

All down the waterway, craft moved. Farro Westerby stood at the forward port of his aquataxi, staring ahead and ignoring the water traffic moving by him. His two fellow Isolationists stood slightly apart, not speaking. Farro's eye was on the rising structure on the left bank ahead. When the aquataxi moored as near to this structure as possible, Farro stepped ashore; glancing back impatiently, he waited for one of his companions to pay the fare.

"Wonderful, isn't it?" the taxi man said, nodding toward the strange building as he cast off. "I can't ever see us putting up anything like it."

"No," Farro said flatly, walking away ahead of his friends.

They had disembarked in that sector of the capital called Horby Clive Island. Located in the government center of New Union, most of it had been ceded to the Galactics a year earlier. In that brief time, using Earth labor for the rough work, they had transformed the place. Six of their large, irregular buildings were already completed. The seventh was now going up, creating a new wonder for the world.

"We will wait here for you, Farro," one of the two men said, extending his hand formally. "Good fortune with the Galactic Minister. As the only Isolationist with an extensive knowledge of the Galactic tongue, Galingua, you represent, as you know, our best chance of putting our case for Earth's remaining outside the Multiplanet Federation."

As Farro thanked him and accepted the proffered hand, the other man, a stooping septuagenarian with a pale voice, gripped Farro's arm.

"And the case is clear enough," he said. "These aliens pretend they offer us federation out of altruism. Most people swallow that, because they believe Earth ingenuity must be a valuable asset anywhere in the galaxy. So it may be, but we Isolationists claim there must be some ulterior motive for a superior race's wanting to welcome in a junior one as they appear to welcome us. If you can get a hint from this Minister Jandanagger as to what that motive is, you'll have done more than well."

"Thank you. I think I have the situation pretty clear," Farro said sharply, regretting his tone of voice at once. But the other two were wise enough to make allowance for nervousness in time of stress. When he left them to make his way toward the Galactic buildings, their faces held only sincere smiles of farewell.

As Farro pushed through the crowds of sightseers who stood here all day watching the new building develop, he listened with interest and some contempt for their comments. Many of them were discussing the current announcement on federation.

"I think their sincerity is proved by the way they've let us join. It's nothing but a friendly gesture."

"It shows what respect they must have for Earth."

"You can't help seeing the future's going to be wonderful, now that we can export goods all over the galaxy. I tell you, we're in for a boom all around."

"Which goes to prove that however advanced the race, they can't do without the good old Earth know-how. Give the Galactics the credit for spotting that!"

The seventh building, around which so many idle spectators clustered, was nearing completion. It grew organically like some vast succulent plant, springing from a flat metal matrix, thrusting along curved girders, encompassing them. Its color was a natural russet, which seemed to take its tones from the sky overhead.

Grouped around the base of this extraordinary structure were distilleries, sprays, excavators and other machines, the function of which was unknown to Farro. They provided the raw material from which the building drew its bulk.

To one side of these seven well-designed eccentricities lay the spacefield. There, too, was another minor mystery. Earth governments had ceded—willingly when they sniffed the prizes to be won from federation—five such centers as that on Horby Clive Island in various parts of the globe. Each center was being equipped as a spaceport and educational unit in which terrestrials would learn to understand the antiphonal complexities of Galingua and to behave as citizens of a well-populated galaxy.

Even granting vast alien resources, it was a formidable project. According to estimates, at least eight thousand Galactics were working on Earth. Yet on the spacefield sat but one craft, an unlikely looking polyhedron with Arcturan symbols on its hull. The Galactics, in short, seemed to have remarkably few spaceships.

That was a point he would like to investigate, Farro thought, speculatively eying the inert beacons around the perimeter of the field.

He skirted them, avoiding the crowds as far as possible, and arrived at the entrance to one of the other six Galactic buildings, quite as eccentric in shape as its unfinished brother. As he walked in, an Earthman in dark-gray livery came deferentially forward.

"I have an appointment with Galactic Minister Jandanagger Laterobinson," Farro announced, pronouncing the strange name awkwardly. "I am Farro Westerby, special deputy of the Isolationist League."

As soon as he heard the phrase Isolationist League, the receptionist's manner chilled. Setting his lips, he beckoned Farro over to a small side apartment, the doors of which closed as Farro entered. The apartment, the Galactic equivalent of an elevator, began to move through the building, traveling upward on what Farro judged to be an elliptical path. It delivered him into Jandanagger Laterobinson's room.

Standing up, the Galactic Minister greeted Farro with amiable reserve, giving the latter an opportunity to sum up his opponent. Laterobinson was unmistakably humanoid; he might, indeed, have passed for an Earthman, were it not for the strangeness of his eyes, set widely apart in his face and half hidden by the peculiar configuration of an epicanthic fold of skin. This minor variation of feature gave to Jandanagger what all his race seemed to possess: a watchful, tensely withdrawn air.

"You know the reason for my visit, Minister," Farro said, when he had introduced himself. He spoke carefully in Galingua, the language he had spent so many months so painfully learning; initially, its wide variation in form from any terrestrial tongue had all but baffled him.

"Putting it briefly, you represent a body of people who fear contact with the other races in the Galaxy—unlike most of your fellows on Earth," Jandanagger said easily. Expressed like that, the idea sounded absurd.

"I would rather claim to represent those who have thought more deeply about the present situation than perhaps their fellows have done."

"Since your views are already known to me through the newly established Terrestrial-Galactic Council, I take it you wish us to discuss this matter personally?"

"That is so."

Jandanagger returned to his chair, gesturing Farro into another.

"My role on Earth is simply to talk and to listen," he said, not without irony. "So do please feel free to talk."

"Minister, I represent five per cent of the people of Earth. If this sounds a small number, I would point out that that percentage contains some of the most eminent men in the world. Our position is relatively simple. You first visited Earth over a year ago, at the end of Ishrail's decade of exile; after investigation, you decided we were sufficiently advanced to become probationary members of the Galactic Federation. As a result, certain advantages and disadvantages will naturally accrue; although both sides will reap advantages, we shall suffer all the disadvantages—and they may well prove fatal to us."

Pausing, he scrutinized Jandanagger, but nothing was to be learned from the Minister's continued look of friendly watchfulness. He continued speaking.

"Before I deal with these disadvantages, may I protest against what will seem to you perhaps a minor point. You have insisted, your charter insists, that this world shall be arbitrarily renamed; no longer shall it be known as Earth, but as Yinnisfar. Is there any defensible reason why this outlandish name should be adopted?"

The Minister smiled broadly and relaxed, as if the question had given him the key he needed to the man sitting opposite him. A bowl of New Union sweets lay on his desk; he pushed them across to Farro and, when the latter refused, took a sugary lump and bit it before replying.

"About three hundred planets calling themselves Earth are known to us," he said. "Any new claimants to the title are automatically rechristened upon federation. From now on you are Yinnisfar. However, I think it would be more profitable if we discussed the advantages and disadvantages of federation, if that is what you wish to talk about."

Farro sighed and resigned himself.

"Very well," he said. "To begin with, the advantages to you. You will have here a convenient base, dock and administrative seat in a region of space you say you have yet to explore and develop. Also, it is possible that when arrangements are worked out between us, terrestrials may be engaged to help colonize the new worlds you expect to find in this region. We shall be a cheap manufacturing area for you. We shall produce such items as plastics, clothes, foodstuffs and simple tools which it will be easier for you to buy from us than transport from your distant home planets. Is this correct?"

"As you point out, Mr. Westerby, Earth occupies a key position in the Federation's present thousand-year plan for expansion. Although at present you can only regard yourselves as a frontier world, at the end of that period you may well be a key world. At the end of ten thousand years—well, your peoples are full of confidence; the omens are good."

"In short, there is promotion ahead if we behave ourselves?"

The acid note in Farro's voice merely brought a slight smile to Jandanagger's lips.

"One is not made head boy in one's first few days at school."

"Let me then enumerate the advantages, as opposed to the promises, which Earth will enjoy from entering your Federation. In the first place, we shall enjoy material benefits: new machines, new toys, new gadgets and some new techniques like your vibro-molecular system of building—which produces, if I may say so, some excruciatingly ugly structures."

"One's tastes, Mr. Westerby, have to be trained to appreciate anything of aesthetic worth."

"Quite. Or to regard the hideous as normal. However, that brings us to the nonmaterial assets inherent in belonging to

your Federation. You plan to revolutionize our educational
systems. From nursery school to university, you will incul-
cate mores, matters and methods foreign to us; Earth will
be invaded not by soldiers but by teachers—which is the
surest way of gaining a bloodless victory."

The wide eyes regarded Farro calmly, but still as if from
behind a barricade.

"How else are we to help Yinnisfarians become citizens
of a complex civilization? For a start, it is essential your
people learn Galingua. Education is a science and an art for
which you have not yet begun to formulate the rules. The
whole question is enormously complicated, and quite beyond
brief explanation—not that I could explain it, for I am not
an educational specialist; those specialists will arrive here
when my work is done and the formal membership charters
are signed. But to take just one simple point. Your children
first go to school at, say, five years old. They go into a
class with other children and are separated from their homes;
learning becomes at once an isolated part of life, something
done in certain hours. And their first lesson is to obey the
teacher. Thus, if their education is rated a success, it is because, to whatever extent, they have learned obedience and
forfeited independence of mind; and they are probably set
at permanent odds with their home environment.

"Our methods differ radically. We allow no children to
enter our schools before the age of ten—but by that time,
thanks to certain instructive toys and devices they have been
familiar with for years, they will come knowing at least as
much as your child at school-leaving age. And not only knowing—behaving, feeling, understanding."

Farro was at a disadvantage.

"I feel like a heathen being told by a missionary that I
should be wearing clothes."

The other man smiled, got up, and came over to him.

"Be consoled that that's a false analogy," he said. "You
are *demanding* the clothes. And when you wear them, you
are certain to admire the cut."

All of which, Farro reflected, made the two of them no
less heathen and missionary.

"Don't look so disconcerted, Mr. Westerby. You have a
perfect right to be distressed at the thought of your planet
being depersonalized. But that is something we would not
dream of doing. Depersonalized, you are nothing to yourselves or us. We need worlds capable of making their best

personal contribution. If you would care to come with me, I should like to give you perhaps a better idea of how the civilized galaxy functions."

Farro rose to his feet. It consoled him that he was slightly taller than the Minister. Jandanagger stood courteously aside, ushered his guest through a door. As they walked down a silent corridor, Farro found his tongue again.

"I haven't fully explained why I think that federation would be such a bad thing for Earth. We are progressing on our own. Eventually, we shall develop our own method of space travel, and come to join you on a more equal footing."

Jandanagger shook his head.

"Space travel—travel between different star systems—is not just a matter of being able to build starships. Any post-nuclear culture can stumble on that trick. Space travel is a state of mind. The journey's always hell, and you never find a planet, however lovely, that suits you as well as the one on which you were born. You need an incentive."

"What sort of incentive?"

"Have you any idea?"

"I take it you are not referring to interstellar trading or conquest?"

"Correct."

"I'm afraid I don't know what sort of an incentive you mean."

The Minister gave something like a chuckle and said, "I'll try and show you presently. You were going to tell me why federation would be a bad thing for Earth."

"No doubt it has been to your purpose to learn something of our history, Minister. It is full of dark things. Blood; war; lost causes; forgotten hopes; ages in chaos and days when even desperation died. It is no history to be proud of. Though many men individually seek good, collectively they lose it as soon as it is found. Yet we have one quality which always gives cause for hope that tomorrow may be better: initiative. Initiative has never faded, even when we crawled from what seemed the last ditch.

"But if we know that there exists a collective culture of several thousand worlds which we can never hope to emulate, what is to prevent us from sinking back into despair forever?"

"An incentive, of course."

As he spoke, Jandanagger led the way into a small, boomerang-shaped room with wide windows. They sank onto a low couch, and at once the room moved. The dizzy view from the window shifted and rolled beneath them. The room was airborne.

"This is our nearest equivalent to your trains. It runs on a nucleonically bonded track. We are going only as far as the next building; there is some equipment I would like you to inspect."

No reply seemed to be required, and Farro sat silent. He had known an electric moment of fear when the room first moved. In no more than ten seconds they swooped to the branch of another Galactic building, becoming part of it.

Once more leading the way, Jandanagger escorted him to an elevator, which took them down into a basement room. They had arrived. The equipment of which Jandanagger had spoken was not particularly impressive in appearance. Before a row of padded seats ran a counter, above which a line of respirator-like masks hung, with several cables trailing from them into the wall.

The Galactic Minister seated himself, motioning Farro into an adjoining seat.

"What is this apparatus?" Farro asked, unable to keep a slight tinge of anxiety from his tone.

"It is a type of wave-synthesizer. In effect, it renders down many of the wave lengths which man cannot detect by himself, translating them into paraphrased terms which he can. At the same time, it feeds in objective and subjective impressions of the universe. That is to say, you will experience— when you wear the mask and I switch it on—instrumental recordings of the universe—visual and aural and so on—as well as human impressions of it.

"I should warn you that owing to your lack of training, you may unfortunately gather a rather confused impression from the synthesizer. All the same, I fancy that it will give you a better rough idea of what the galaxy is like than you would get from a long star journey."

"Let's go," Farro said, clutching his cold hands together.

Now the entire column of lemmings had embarked into the still water. They swam smoothly and silently, their communal wake soon dissolving into the grandly gentle motion of the sea. Gradually the column attenuated as the stronger animals drew farther ahead and the weaker ones dropped behind. One by one, inevitably, these weaker animals drowned; yet, until their sleek heads finally disappeared below the surface, they still pressed forward with bulging eyes fixed upon the far and empty horizon.

No human spectator, however devoid of anthropomorphic feeling, could have failed to ask himself what might be the nature of the goal that prompted such a sacrifice.

The inside of the mask was cold. It fitted loosely over his face, covering his ears and leaving only the back of his head free. Again a touch of unreasoning fear shot through him.

"The switch is by your hand," the Minister said. "Press it."

Ferro pressed the switch. Darkness submerged him.

"I am with you," the Minister said steadily. "I have a mask on, too, and can see and feel what you do."

A spiral curled out into the darkness, boring its way through nothing—an opaque, smothering nothing as warm as flesh. Materializing from the spiral there issued a cluster of bubbles, dark as polyhedric grapes, multiplying and multiplying as if breathed from an inexhaustible bubble pipe. The lights on their surfaces, glittering, changing, spun a misty web which gradually veiled the operation.

"Cells are being formed, beaten out in endless duplication on the microscopic anvils of creation. You witness the beginning of a new life," Jandanagger said, his voice sounding distant.

Like a curtain by an open window, the cells trembled behind their veil, awaiting life. The moment of its coming was not perceptible. It was only that now the veil had something to conceal within itself; its translucence dimmed, its surface patterned, a kind of blind purpose shaped it into more definite outline. No longer was it beautiful.

Consciousness simmered inside it, a pinpoint of instinct-plus without love or knowledge, an eye trying to see through a lid of skin. It was not inert; instead, it struggled on the verge of terror, undergoing the trauma of coming into being, fighting, scrabbling, lest it fall back again into the endless gulf of not-being.

"Here is the afterlife your religions tell of," Jandanagger's voice said. "This is the purgatory every one of us must undergo, only it comes not after but before life. The spirit that will become us has to tread the billion years of the past before it reaches the present it can be born into. One might almost say there was something it had to expiate."

The fetus was all Farro's universe; it filled the mask, filled him. He suffered with it, for it obviously suffered. Pressures racked it, the irremediable pressures of time and biochemistry, the pain of which it strove to lessen by changing shape. It writhed from wormhood to slughood, it grew gills and a tail. Fishlike, and then no longer fishlike, it toiled up the steep slope of evolution, mouselike, piglike, apelike, babylike.

"This is the truth the wisest man forgets—that he has done all this."

Now the environment changed. The fetus, exerting itself, had become a baby, and the baby could only become a man by the proddings of a thousand new stimuli. And all these stimuli—animal, vegetable, or mineral—lived too, in their different way. They competed. They inflicted constant challenges on the man creature; some of them, semisentient, invaded his flesh and bred there, creating their own life cycles; others, nonsentient, were like waves that passed unceasingly through his mind and his body. He seemed hardly an entity, merely a focal point of forces, constantly threatened with dissolution.

So complete was the identification between the image and the receiver that Farro felt he was the man. He recognized that everything happening to the man happened to him; he sweated and writhed like the fetus, conscious of the salt water in his blood, the unstoppable rays in the marrow of his bones. Yet the mind was freer than it had been in the fetus stage; during the wrenching moment of fear when environments had changed, the eye of consciousness had opened its lids.

"And now the man changes environments again, to venture away from his own planet," the Galactic Minister said.

But space was not space as Farro had reckoned it. It struck his eyes like slate: not a simple nothingness, but an unfathomable web of forces, a creeping blend of stresses and fields in which stars and planets hung like dew amid spiders' webs. No life was here, only the same interaction of planes and pressures that had attended the man all along, and of which even the man himself was composed. Nonetheless, his perceptions reached a new stage, the light of consciousness burned more steadily.

Again he was reaching out, swimming toward the confines of his Galaxy. About him, proportions changed, slid, dwindled. In the beginning, the womb had been everywhere, equipped with all the menace and coercion of a full-scale universe; now the galaxy was revealed as smaller than the womb—a pint-sized goldfish bowl in which a tiddler swam, unaware of the difference between air and water. For there was no spanning the gulfs between galaxies: there lay nothing, the nothing of an unremitting Outside. And the man had never met nothing before. Freedom was not a condition he knew, because it did not exist in his interpenetrated existence.

As he swam up to the surface, something stirred beyond the yellow rim of the Galaxy. The something could hardly be seen; but it was there on the Outside, wakeful and clawed, a creature with senses, though insensate. It registered half as sight, half as noise: a smoldering and delayed series of pops, like the sound of bursting arteries. It was big. Farro screamed into the blackness of his mask at its bigness and its anger.

The creature was waiting for the man. Stretching, it stretched right around the Galaxy, around the goldfish bowl, its supernatant bat's wings groping for purchase.

Farro screamed again.

"I'm sorry," he said weakly, as he felt the Minister removing his mask for him. "I'm sorry."

The Minister patted his shoulder. Shuddering, Farro buried his face in his hands, trying to erase the now loathsome contact of the mask. That thing beyond the Galaxy—it seemed to have entered and found a permanent place in his mind.

At last, gathering himself together, he stood up. Weakness floated in every layer of him. Moistening his lips, he spoke.

"So you inveigle us into the Federation to face that!"

Jandanagger took his arm.

"Come back to my room. There is a point I can now make clear to you which I could not before. Earth has not been inveigled into the Federation. With your Earthbound eyes, I know how you see the situation. You fancy that despite the evidence before your eyes of Galactic superiority, there must be some vital point on which Earth can offer something unbeatable. You fancy there must be some factor for which we need terrestrial help—a factor it does not yet suit us to reveal—isn't that so?"

Farro avoided the other's narrow eyes as they ascended in an elevator to the top of the building.

"There are other things beside the material ones," he said evasively. "Think for instance of the great heritage of literature in the world; to a truly civilized race, that might appear invaluable."

"That depends upon what you mean by civilized. The senior races of the Galaxy, having lost any taste for the spectacle of mental suffering, would be unlikely to find much attraction in your literatures."

This gently administered rebuke silenced Farro. After a pause, the Galactic Minister continued. "No, you have no secret virtues, alas, for which we are gulling you into the Federation. The boot is on the other foot. We are taking you in as a duty, because you need looking after. I apologize for putting the matter so bluntly; but such may be the best way."

Stopping gently, the elevator released them into the boomerang-shaped room. In a minute, they were speeding back to the building Farro had first entered, with the crowded Horby Clive sector below them. Farro closed his eyes, still sick and shattered. The implications of what Jandanagger had said were momentarily beyond his comprehension.

"I understand nothing," he said. "I don't understand why it should be your duty to look after Earth."

"Then already you do begin to understand," Jandanagger said, and for the first time personal warmth tempered his voice. "For not only are our sciences beyond yours, so are our philosophies and thought disciplines. All our mental abilities have been keyed semantically into the language in which you have learned to converse with me—Galingua."

The flying room was reabsorbed; they became again merely one leaf tip of a giant building growing toward the gray clouds.

"Your language is certainly comprehensive and complex," Farro said, "but perhaps my knowledge of it is too elementary for me to recognize the extra significance of which you speak."

"That is only because you have still to be shown how Galingua is more than a language, how it is a way of life, our means of space travel itself! Concentrate on what I am telling you, Mr. Westerby."

Confusedly, Farro shook his head as the other spoke; blood seemed to be congested at the base of his skull. The odd idea came to him that he was losing his character, his identity. Wisps of meaning, hints of a greater comprehension, blew through his brain like streamers in the draft of a fan. As he tried to settle them, keep them steady, his own language became less like the bedrock of his being; his knowledge of Galingua, coupled with the experiences of the last hour, gradually assumed a dominant tone. With Jandanagger's grave eyes upon him, he began to think in the tongue of the Galaxy.

For Jandanagger was talking, and with increasing rapidity. Although his meanings seemed clear, it felt to Farro as if they were being comprehended only by a level below his conscious one. It was like partial drunkenness, when the grand simplicities of the world are revealed in wine and the mind skates over the thin ice of experience.

For Jandanagger was talking of many things at once, shifting things that could not be spoken of in terrestrial tongues, dissolving mental disciplines never formulated through terrestrial voices. Yet all these things balanced together in one sentence like jugglers' balls, enhancing each other.

For Jandanagger was talking of only one thing: the thrust of creation. He spoke of what the synthesizer had demonstrated: that man was never a separate entity, merely a solid within a solid—or, better still, a flux within a flux. That he had only a subjective identity. That the wheeling matter of the Galaxy was one with him.

And he spoke in the same breath of Galingua, which was merely a vocal representation of that flux, and whose cadences followed the great spiral of life within the flux. As he spoke, he unlocked the inner secret of it to Farro, so that what before had been a formal study became an orchestration, with every cell another note.

With a wild exultation, Farro was able to answer now, merging with the spiral of talk. The new language was like a great immaterial stupa, its base broad, rooted in the ground of the ego, its spire high, whirling up into the sky. And by it, Farro gradually ascended with Jandanagger; or, rather, the proportions and perspectives about him changed, slid, dwindled, as they had done in the synthesizer. With no sense of alarm, he found himself high above the gaping crowds, shooting upward on an etheric spiral.

Within him was a new understanding of the stresses permeating all space. He rode upward through the planes of the universe, Jandanagger close by, sharing the revelation.

Now it was clear why the Galactics needed few space ships. Their big, polygonal vessels carried only material; man himself had found a safer way of traveling in the goldfish bowl of the Galaxy.

Looking outward, Farro saw where the stars thinned. Out there was the thing with claws, popping silently like bursting blood vessels. Fear came to him again.

"The thing in the synthesizer . . ." he said to Jandanagger, through the new-found medium of communication. "The thing that surrounds the Galaxy—if man can never get out, cannot it get in at us?"

For a long minute Jandanagger was silent, searching for the key phrases of explanation.

"You have learned as much as you have very rapidly," he said. "By not-understanding and then by well-understanding, you have made yourself one of the true citizens of the Galaxy. But you have only taken leap X; now you must take leap X^{10}. Prepare yourself."

"I am prepared."

"All that you have learned is true. Yet there is a far greater truth, a truer truth. Nothing exists in the ultimate sense: all is illusion, a two-dimensional shadow play on the mist of space-time. Yinnisfar itself means 'illusion.' "

"But the clawed thing . . ."

"The clawed thing is why we fare ever farther ahead into the illusion of space. *It* is real. Only the Galaxy as you previously misinterpreted it is unreal, being but a configuration of mental forces. That monster, that thing you sensed, is the residue of the slime of the evolutionary past still lingering—not outside you, but *in your own mind*. It is from that we must escape. We must grow from it."

More explanation followed, but it was beyond Farro. In a flash, he saw that Jandanagger, with an eagerness to experiment, had driven him too far and too fast. He could not make the last leap; he was falling back, toppling into not-being. Somewhere within him, the pop-thud-pop sound of bursting arteries began. Others would succeed where he had failed, but, meanwhile, the angry claws were reaching from the heavens for him—to sunder, not to rescue.

And now the lemmings were scattered over a considerable area of sea. Few of the original column were left; the remaining swimmers, isolated from each other, were growing tired. Yet they pressed forward as doggedly as ever toward the unseen goal.

Nothing was ahead of them. They had launched themselves into a vast—but not infinite—world without landmarks. The cruel incentive urged them always on. And if an invisible spectator had asked himself the agonized Why to it all, an answer might have occurred to him: that these creatures were not heading for some special promise in their future, but merely fleeing from some terrible fear in their past.

THE
MUTANT
MILLENNIA

To see the universe, and see it whole . . . Nothing in it was man's, yet at that time it could only appear that he had inherited it. For Earth itself—or Yinnisfar, as it was henceforth called—nothing but buoyant optimism suited the day. Terrestrials, having been granted federation, now possessed Galingua, which looked like the ultimate key to everything.

They sped out into a Galaxy peculiarly vulnerable to new forces. As has been observed, galactic civilization had reached a point of stasis; though its resources were inexhaustible, its initiative was not. The patterns of the Self-perpetuating War wove unceasing artistries of circumstance capable of carrying whole societies along in a mirage of meaningful existence. The Yinnisfarians did not burst, therefore, into a dynamic system but into a glorified Land of Nod.

The results might have been predicted. Over the next six hundred generations, Yinnisfarians amassed more and more power to themselves. By peaceful means, or by means little better than piracy, they worked their way into the highest galactic positions, succeeding less through their own intrinsic superiority than through the indifference of their rivals. This was a halcyon age, the age of the fulfillment of Yinnisfar.

As the years passed, and Yinnisfar conquered by commerce, its attitudes insensibly underwent a modification. Then came the blow that forced man to alter his attitude toward himself. His metaphysical view of being had of course been continually subject to change; but now the terrible moment arrived when he was revealed to himself in an entirely new light, as an alien, in a hostile environment.

It is useful that this next fragment reminds us incidentally that if the universe appeared to rest in human hands, humanity was never alone or unregarded. There were always things that could see though they had no faces and understand though they had no brains.

IT WAS ONE OF THOSE UNLIKELY ACCIDENTS THAT ARE LIKELY
to occur anywhere. The undersea trawler *Bartlemeo* was approaching the subport of Capverde at four hundred and ninety fathoms when it developed engine trouble. I am not a
technical man, so that I cannot exactly describe the fault;
apparently uranium slugs move slowly through the piles of
these ships, and the dispensing mechanism which shoots the
used slugs into the separators became jammed. Instead of
using manual remote control to tackle the fault, the chief
engineer, a man called Je Regard, went in himself to clear the
slugway. As he climbed through the inspection hatches,
Regard snagged his protective suit on a latch without notic-
ing it. He was able to repair the congestion in the slugway
without trouble, but collapsed as he emerged again, having
collected a near-lethal dose of radiation in his kidneys.

The *Bartlemeo* carried no doctor. A general call for one
was sent out immediately.

I have said I am no technician; neither am I a philoso-
pher. Yet I can see in this trivial episode which began so
many centuries of trouble the pattern of all great things
which start as something fairly insignificant.

In the midst of the shifting and immemorial sands of the
Sara Desert crouches the Ahaggari plateau, breasting the dunes
like a liner in a sullen sea. On the edge of the plateau stands
Barbe Barber, the Institute of Medical Meditation, an elaborate and ancient building in the grand fifty-first epoch manner, as fugal as Angkor Wat, as uncompromising as the
Lunar Enterventual. Set about with palms, which lend shade
to its wide, paved walks, Barbe Barber thrusts its towers and
upper stories above the trees to scan the mighty continent
on which it stands—just as its occupants, the doctors, scan
the interior of the body, the inner continent of man.

Gerund Gyres, neckcloth perpetually mopping his brow,
stood before the main steps of the institute, waiting. His aircar, which had brought him, stood some distance off in the
park. He waited humbly in the rocking heat, although he
was a proud man; no layman was ever allowed in Barbe Barber.

At length the figure Gerund expected to see appeared at
the top of the wide steps. It was his wife, Cyro. She turned
back, as if to bid someone behind her farewell, and then
commenced to descend the steps. As always when Gerund
met her here, he was conscious of how Cyro, as she came

down those steps, had to force her mind out from the cloister of Barbe Barber back into the external world. While he watched with anxiety and love, the curve of her back straightened, her head came up, her pace increased. By the time she reached Gerund, her eyes held that familiar expression of detached amusement with which she faced both life and her husband.

"It feels like weeks since I saw you," Cyro said, kissing Gerund on the mouth and putting her arms around him.

"It *is* weeks," he protested.

"Is it really?" she said playfully. "It doesn't seem as long!"

Gerund took her hand and led her around to the massive triangle that was their aircar. The month of meditation which Cyro, as a doctor, was compelled to undergo every year was undoubtedly beneficial for her; based on high-ega systems, the disciplines of Barbe Barber were courses of refreshment for brains and bodies of the medical fraternities of the world. Cyro looked younger and more vital than ever; Gerund told himself that, after six years of marriage, he was less a source of vitality in his wife's life than was high-ega; but it was irrational to hope for any change in that respect.

Walking together they reached the aircar. Jeffy, their bonded servant, was leaning against the metal hull, awaiting them, arms patiently folded.

"It's nice to see you again, Doctor Cyro," he said, opening the door for them and standing back.

"And you, Jeffy. You're looking brown."

"Baked right through," he said, smiling broadly. His homeland was a bleak Northern island lying under frost most of the year; equatorial tour suited him well. Though it was thirty years since he had been brought from that distant land, Jeffy still spoke its simple patois, Ingulesh; he had been unable to acquire the Galingua in which Gerund, Cyro, and most civilized people of the day thought and conversed.

They climbed into their seats, Jeffy taking the pilot's throne. He was a great, slow man who moved purposefully. His sluggish mentality had left him fit for nothing but the role of a bonded servant, yet he handled the heavy flier with delicacy.

Jeffy now brought them over to one of the semicircular take-off collars which would absorb their exhaust gases. The orange signal came through on the collar beacon and they burst immediately into vertical flight. At once the trees and the white-and-gray walls of Barbe Barber dwindled away be-

low them, as inconsiderable as a child's charade between the
limitless sandwich of sky and sand. The plane headed due
west, on a course that would bring them eventually to the
Gyreses' home in the Puterska Islands—or would have
brought them there but for the sick man a thousand meters
under the bland surface of the Lanic Sea, a sick man of whose
very existence they were as yet unaware.

"Well, Gerund, what has happened in the world since I've
been out of it?" Cyro asked, settling herself carefully opposite her husband.

"Nothing very exciting. The Dualists wish to register every
planet in the Federation. The Barrier Research City has been
opened with due pomp. And the world of learning is at log-
gerheads over Pamlira's new work, *Paraevolution*."

"I must certainly read it," Cyro said, with a trace of excitement. "What's his theory this time?"

"It's one of those things that don't summarize easily,"
Gerund told her, "but briefly Pamlira accepts the Pla-To position of the Dual Theory and claims that evolution is working toward greater consciousness. Plants are less conscious
than animals, animals less conscious than men, and men
came after the animals which came after the plants. Plants,
animals, men, are only first steps in a long ladder. Pamlira
points out that man is by no means fully conscious. He
sleeps, he forgets, he is unaware of the workings of his
body—"

"Which is why we doctors exist," Cyro inserted.

"Exactly. As Pamlira himself says, only certain unusual
individuals, associated together into our present Orders of
Medicine, can to some extent participate consciously in somatic activity."

She smiled a neutral smile.

"And where does he go from there?" she asked.

"He postulates that the next evolutionary step would be
something—a being—conscious in every cell; and that Nature may be already preparing to usher it onto the stage. The
time, apparently, is ripe for the new being."

"Already?" She raised a quizzical eyebrow. "I should have
thought he was a few million years early! Have all the
permutations of which man is capable been played through
already?"

"Pamlira spends half the book explaining why the new
species is due," Gerund said. "According to him, evolution
accelerates like scientific progress; the more protoplasm avail-

able for modification, the sooner the modification appears. On thirty thousand planets, you have quite a weight of protoplasm."

Cyro was silent. With a slight ache in his heart, Gerund noticed that she asked him nothing about his personal opinion of Pamlira's book, though it must have been clear from what he said that he had read it. She would consider that his opinion as an industrial ecologist was not worth having, and refuse to yield enough to convention to ask him anyway.

Finally Cyro said, "Whatever this superconscious new species might be, man would give it little chance to establish its supremacy—or even to survive. It would be blotted out before it had a chance to multiply. After all, we could hardly be expected to be hospitable to the usurpers of our comfortable place in the cosmos."

"Pamlira says," Gerund told her, "that evolution would take care of that if it really wanted man out of the way. The new species would be given some sort of defense—or weapon—to render it invulnerable against the species it would be superseding."

"How?" she asked indignantly, as if he had said something stupid. "Evolution is a completely neutral—blind—process."

"That's what worries Pamlira!" Gerund said. He could see she considered this remark superficial. So it was; it had been designed to cover his uncertainty of what Pamlira had actually said on that point. *Paraevolution* was stiff reading; Gerund had only waded through it for Cyro's sake, because he knew the subject would interest her.

Paraevolution and its attendant woes were to be driven out of both their minds. Jeffy appeared, framed bulkily in the door dividing the control room from the cabin, while the aircar roared on above the Sara on autopilot.

"There's a call coming in for a doctor," he said, trundling his words out one by one. "It's coming from Capverde subport, almost dead ahead. They've got an underseaman in urgent need of healing." He looked at Cyro as he spoke.

"Of course I'll take it," she said, getting up and brushing past him into the control room.

The call was coming through again as she reached the wireless. She listened carefully to it, and then answered.

"Thank you, Doctor Gyres," the Capverde operator said relievedly. "We'll wait for your arrival."

They were now only some six hundred miles from the Capverde Islands; already they had covered nearly twice that distance from Barbe Barber. Even as Cyro left the wireless, the Lanic Sea showed ahead. On this desolate stretch of the continental coast, the saddest on Yinnisfar for all its blinding sun, the desert stretched right to the water's edge—or, to take it conversely, the beach extended from here to Barbe Barber. They flashed across the dividing line between sand and sea and headed WSW. Almost at once, cloud formed like a floor below them, blotting out the turning globe.

Within ten minutes, checking his instruments, Jeffy took them down, finally skimming under low nimbo-stratus to find the fourteen islands of the Capverde archipelago to their left ahead.

"Nicely calculated," Gerund said. Jeffy played the metal think-box like a child genius conjuring Britziparbtu from a cello-organ; he had that flair for machines only granted to the half-witted.

The aircar banked to port around Satago and plunged toward the sea, dropping vertically. The gray waters came up to meet them like a smack in the face, boiled around them, swallowed them, and the altimeter finger on the instrument panel, swooping past the Zero sign, began to read fathoms instead of feet.

Jeffy was in radio contact with the subport again. Beacons at ten-fathom intervals lit their way down to the underwater city. Finally a hangar, poised above a hundred-fathom gulf, loomed whale's-mouth wide in front of them; they jetted in and the jaws closed behind them. Powerful valves immediately began to suck the water from the hangar, replacing it with air.

Already mentally composing herself for what was to come, Cyro was out of the flier before the dock hand on the vacobile could collect the trapped fish and blow the floor dry. Gerund and Jeffy were left to follow as best they could.

Outside the hangar, two port officials greeted Cyro.

"Thank you for coming so quickly, Doctor Gyres," one of them said. "They probably told you the details of the case on the wireless. It's the chief engineer of the undersea trawler *Bartlemeo* who's in trouble. . . ."

As he related the cogent facts of the case, the official ushered Cyro, Gerund and Jeffy aboard a small, open vehicle. The other official drove, and they sped along the strange waterfront where, despite all the usual bustle connected with a dock, no water could be seen.

For ages, the human species had regarded the seas as either a perilous highway or a suitable place in which they could make hit-and-run raids on shoals of fish; then, belatedly, it had taken the oceans in hand and tended them with the same care it bestowed on the land; now they were farmed rather than fished. As more and more personnel turned to work on the savannas of the deep, so the subports had grown up, underwater towns that paid little homage to their softer counterparts on dry land.

Capverde subport, because of its favored position in the Lanic and its proximity to Little Union, the second greatest of Yinnisfar's cities, had been one of the first such ports to be established. The quarter of the city in which the open machine now stopped was more than ten centuries old. The hospital into which they were ushered presented a crumbling façade.

Inside were the monastic arrangements usual to hospitals everywhere. From a cloister, doors gave onto a waiting room, a primitive kitchen, a radio room, small cells; in one of the cells lay Je Regard, chief engineer of the *Bartlemeo,* with a dose of hard radiation in his kidneys.

An ancient bondman, bent and gray-bearded, announced himself as Laslo; he was on duty. Apart from him and the sick man, the musty-smelling place was empty.

"See what you can do for the poor fellow, doctor," one of the officials said, shaking Cyro's elegant hand as he prepared to depart. "I expect the captain of the *Bartlemeo* will call through soon. Meanwhile, we will leave you in peace."

"Thank you," Cyro said, a little blankly, her mind already far from them. She turned away, went into the sick man's cell and closed the door behind her.

For some time after she had gone and the officials had left, Gerund and Jeffy stood aimlessly in the cloister. Jeffy wandered to the archway and looked out at the street. Occasionally a bonded man or woman passed, looking neither to the right nor to the left. The dully lighted fronts of the buildings, many of them carved from the rock, looked like the dwellings of the dead.

Jeffy wrapped his great arms about his torso.

"I want to go home," he said. "It's cold here."

A bead of moisture fell from the roof overhead and

splashed on his cheek. "It's cold and *damp* here," he added.

The gray-bearded guard regarded him speechlessly with a sardonic eye. For a long while there was no more speech. They waited almost without thought, their level of consciousness as dim as the lights outside.

As soon as Cyro Gyres entered the cell, she climbed onto the bunk with the sick man.

Regard was a heavy fellow. Under the single blanket, his vast frame labored up and down with the effort of breathing. The stubble on his face thrust up through three great, pallid jowls. Lying beside him, Cyro felt like Mahomet visiting the mountain.

That the mountain was unconscious only made Cyro's task easier. She placed her bare arm over Regard's bare arm and closed her eyes. She relaxed her muscles, slowing her breathing rate. This was, of course, all standard professional procedure. Efficiently, Cyro reduced the rate of her heart's beat, concentrating on that vital pulse until it seemed to grow and grow, and she could submerge herself in it.

She was sinking down through a dull red haze, a featureless haze, a haze stretching from pole to pole. But gradually, a mirage forming in a distance, striations appeared through the haze. As her viewpoint sank, it magnified; the islands of the blood slid up to meet her. The islands moved with the clerical purpose of vultures, expanding, changing, ranging, rearranging, and still she moved among them. Though she moved, all sense of direction was entirely shed. Here the dimensions carried no sense of up or down; even near and far were confused to her sight, which was no longer sight.

Not only sight had she lost. Almost every other ability except volition had been stripped from her when she took this plunge into the somatic world of her own bodily universe, as a man throws off all his clothes before diving into a river. She could not think, remember, taste, touch, turn, communicate, or act; yet a shadow of all these things remained with her; much as the dragonfly larva, climbing its reed out of the ooze, carries a vague image of the creature it will become, Cyro had some memory of herself as the individual she had been. And this pale memory stayed with her by dint of the years of training she had received in Medical Meditation at Barbe Barber, otherwise she would have been lost in that most terrible trap of all: the universe of one's own body.

Almost without will, she headed down her bloodstream.

It was swimming—flying? crawling?—through an endless everglade, flooded above the treetops, treacle-thick with fish, minnow, mackerel, mace and manta ray. It was creeping—climbing? drifting?—down a glass canyon, whose walls flickered with more-than-earthly firelight. So, so, until before her loomed a wavering cliff.

The cliff ran around the universe, tall as time, insubstantial as muslin, pock-marked with rabbit holes, through which phantasmic creatures came and went. She drifted through it almost without resistance, like plankton sucked through a sponge.

Now she had passed her lobe of consciousness, her psyche, into Je Regard's arm, into his soma.

Her surroundings were as weird, as strange, as familiar, as they had been before. Submerged on this cellular level, there could be no difference between his body and hers. Yet a difference was there. From the forests of his flesh, strange and always unseen eyes watched her, and a silent and malevolent regard traced her course; for she was an intruder, venturing into the interior of an alien world especially designed to show an intruder no mercy. Little jellies of death twinkled as she passed, and only the confidence of her step held the defending powers at bay.

As she moved on, corpuscles like stars about her, the surrounding activity grew more intense. She was swept along, as by a glutinous current, moving under arches, among branches, past weed tangles, through nets, and the way ahead grew dark and stagnant; though she still drifted forward, the half-live things about her were squirming away, repulsed, flickering with crude blueprints of pain.

She was nearly at the infected kidneys now.

Only the stern disciplines of Medical Meditation now prompted her on. The atmosphere was so thickly repellent that she might have been wallowing in a sewer. But medicine had long ago discovered the powers of self-healing that lie within a body; high-ega and the yogas on which it was founded had pointed the way to releasing those powers. Nowadays, with the psyche of one of the Order of Medicine to spur it on, a patient's body could be made to regenerate itself: to grow a new limb, a new lung, a new liver. The doctors, the modern skin-divers, submerged to marshal the forces of the anatomy against its invaders.

Cyro called to those forces now. About her, layer on layer, horizon high, the cells of the invaded body, each with its thirty thousand genes, lay silent and seemingly deserted. Then, slowly, reluctantly, as her summons persisted, reinforcements came to her, like rats crawling out of a ruined city. *The enemy is ahead!* she pulsed to them, moving forward into the tattered darkness. More and more, they were coming to her cause, lighting the sewer with their internal fires.

Things like little bats hurtled, chittering, out of the heart of the darkness, were struck down, were devoured. And then the enemy launched his assault. He struck with the suddenness of a closing trap.

He was one, he was a million!

He was nothing the textbooks know of—unknown, unknowable.

He fought with laws and powers entirely his own.

He was monstrous, bestial, occult, a greed with fangs, a horned horror, newly hatched. He was so overwhelming that Cyro hardly felt fear: the puissance of the unknown can kill everything but calm in us. She was aware only that a random radioactive particle had struck down and buried itself in a random gene, producing—with a ferocious defiance of the laws of chance—a freak cell, a mutant cell with unfamiliar appetites; nothing in her training prepared her to understand what the appetites were.

Those appetites had lain dormant until *she* approached. *She* had triggered them, woken them. She had breathed her touch of consciousness onto them, and at once the cell had filled with its own awareness. And its awareness was of the desire to conquer.

She could see, feel, hear, sense, that it was tearing through cell after cell, a maniac through empty rooms, filling them with its rebellion. The healing forces about her turned and fled in panic, winging and swimming against a wind which held them helpless. Cyro, too, turned to escape. Her own body was her only refuge, if she could get there.

But the nailed streamers came out of the darkness and wrapped themselves about her. She cracked open her jaws to their toothed extremes, struggling to scream; at once her mouth was filled with sponge, from which little creatures flung themselves and scampered wildly through her being, triumphing. . . .

Gerund and Jeffy sat smoking on a bench under the eyes of the gray-bearded bondman, Laslo. Empty mugs stood beside them; Jeffy had boiled them a hot drink. Now they sat waiting uneasily for Cyro to reappear, their uneasiness growing as the time slipped away.

"I've never known her to take so long on a case before," Gerund said. "Five minutes is generally all she needs. As soon as she has organized the powers of recovery, she comes back."

"This engineer—he sounded pretty bad," Jeffy said.

"Yes, but all the same . . . Five minutes more and I'm going in to see her."

"That's not permitted," declared the graybeard; it was almost the first time he had spoken. What he said was no less than the truth. The etiquette governing doctor and patient was strict, in their own interests; they could not be viewed together, unless by another doctor. Gerund was perfectly familiar with this rule; he had, indeed, a reluctance to see his wife in a trance state, knowing that the sight would only serve to emphasize the constraint he felt between them. All the same, Cyro had been in that room for half an hour; something must be done.

He sat there for two more minutes before getting up and going over to the cell door. Laslo also rose, shouting angrily. As he started to intercept Gerund, Jeffy blocked his way.

"Sit down or I'll pull your nose off," Jeffy said unemotionally. "I'm very strong and I got nothing better to do."

The old man, taking one look into Jeffy's face, went obediently back and sat down. Gerund nodded at his servant, opened the cell door, and slipped inside.

One glance told him that something was wrong—gravely wrong. His wife and the massive engineer lay side by side on a bunk, their arms touching. Their eyes were open, bulging coldly out into space like cod's eyes on a slab, containing no life whatsoever. But their bodies were alive. Every so often, their frames vibrated and bulged and settled again. Cyro's right heel kicked briefly against the bunk, beating a meaningless *rat-tat* on the wooden bed foot. Her skin was gradually suffusing with a crimson blush like a stain; it looked, thought Gerund, as if every shred of flesh in her body had been beaten to a pulp. For a while he stood there transfixed with horror and fear, unable to collect his wits and decide what to do.

A cockroach swarmed up the leg of the bed. It passed within six inches of Je Regard's foot, which protruded bare from under his blanket. As the cockroach moved by, a section of the sole of the foot suddenly grew into a stalk, a dainty thing like a blade of grass; the stalk licked out as quickly as a tongue and caught the cockroach, its legs waving. Gerund slid quietly to the ground in a faint.

Now the flesh on the bed began to change more rapidly. It had organized itself. It slid and smeared out of shape, or flowed in on itself with smacking noises. The cockroach was absorbed. Then, compressing itself, the mass formed back into one human form: Cyro's. Face, body, color of hair, eyes —all became like Cyro's, and every drop of flesh was squeezed into her making. As her last fingernail formed, Gerund rolled over and sat up.

Surprise seized him as he stared about the cell.

It had seemed to him that he had been senseless only a second, yet the sick man had gone! At least Cyro looked better now. She was smiling at him. Perhaps, after all, his anxiety had produced some kind of optical illusion when he entered the cell; perhaps everything was all right. But, on looking more closely at Cyro, his returning sense of re-assurance vanished.

It was uncanny! The person sitting on the bed was Cyro. And yet—and yet—every line of her face, every subtle con-tour Gerund loved so well, had undergone an indefinable transmutation. Even the texture of her flesh had changed. He noticed that her fingers had grown. And there was an-other thing—she was too big. She was too thick and too tall to be Cyro, as she sat on the bed looking at him, trying to smile.

Gerund stood up, faintness threatening to overwhelm him again. He was close to the door. He could run, or he could call for Jeffy, as his instincts bid him.

Instead, he conquered his instincts. Cyro was in trouble, supreme trouble. Here was Gerund's chance, possibly his final one, to prove his devotion to her; if he ran from her now, his chance would have passed forever—or so he told himself, for Gerund could not believe his wife's indifference rested on anything but a distrust of his integrity.

He turned back to her, ignoring her frightfulness.

"Cyro, Cyro, what is wrong?" he asked. "What can I do? Tell me what I can do to help. I'll do anything."

The creature on the bed opened its mouth.

"I shall be better in a minute," it said huskily. The words did not quite coincide with its lip movements.

With a heave, it stood on its feet. It was over seven feet tall, and burly. Gerund stared at it as if hypnotized, but managed with an effort of will to hold out a hand to it. "It's my wife," he told himself, "it's only my wife." But as it lumbered toward him, his nerve broke. The look on its face was too terrible. . . . He turned, too late to get away. It stretched out its arms and caught him almost playfully.

In the cloister, Jeffy was growing bored. For all the affection he bore his master, he found the life of a bond servant a tedious one at times. Under the fishy eye of the old guard, he spread himself along the bench, preparing for a nap; Gerund would call him soon enough when he was wanted.

A bell rang in the radio room.

Casting one last suspicious look at Jeffy, the old man went to answer the call. Jeffy settled back to doze. In a minute, scuffling sounds made him open an eye. A monstrous form, its details lost in the feeble lighting, lumped along on eight or ten legs and vanished into the street. Jeffy was on his feet instantly, a wave of cold horror brushing tenderly over his skin. He turned and made at a run for the sick cell, instinctively connecting this monster with a threat to those he served.

The cell was empty.

"Here, what are you up to?" asked a voice behind him. The graybeard had come up at the sound of Jeffy's footsteps. He peered past Jeffy's elbow into the room. As soon as he saw it was empty, he pulled out a whistle and began to blow wildly on it.

Judge: "You offer as an explanation of the disappearance of your master and mistress the possibility that they may have been—er—devoured by this monster you claim you saw?"

Jeffy: "I didn't say that, sir. I don't know where they went to. I only say I saw this thing slipping out of the hospital, and then they were gone."

Judge: "You have heard that no one else in the subport has seen any such monster. You have heard the evidence of Laslo, the hospital guard, that he saw no such monster. Why, then, do you persist in this tale?"

Jeffy: "I can only say what happened, can't I?"

Judge: "You are *supposed* to say what happened."

Jeffy: "That *is* what happened. It's the truth! I've no secrets, nothing to hide. I was fond of my master. I would never have done away with him—or my mistress."

Judge: "Bonded servants have expressed such sentiments

before, after their masters were dead. If you are innocent of what you are accused of, why did you attempt to escape when old Laslo blew his whistle for the police?"

Jeffy: "I was rattled, sir, do you understand? I was frightened. I'd seen this—thing, and then I'd seen the empty cell, and then that fool started blowing. I—I just hit him without thinking."

Judge: "You do not reveal yourself as a responsible man. We have heard already the witness Laslo's account of the way you threatened him with force soon after you arrived at the hospital."

Jeffy: "And you've heard me tell you why I did so."

Judge: "You realize, I hope, the serious position you are in? You are a simple man, so I will put it to you simply. Under world law, you are charged with the double murder of your master and mistress, and until their bodies are recovered or further evidence comes to light, you are to be housed in our prison."

There were two ways up from the subport to the surface of the Lanic. One way was the sea route, by which both the *Bartlemeo* and the Gyreses' plane had arrived. The other was a land route. An underground funicular railway climbed through three thousand feet of rock from the submerged city to the station in Praia, the capital of the island of Satago. It was by this route that Jeffy was brought to prison.

Overlooking a dusty courtyard sheltered by a baobab, Jeffy's cell window allowed him a glimpse of the sea. It was good to be above ground again, although the cloudy overcast created a greenhouse atmosphere which was particularly oppressive after the cool air of the subport; Jeffy sweated perpetually. He spent a lot of his time standing on his wooden bed, staring out into the heat. Other convicts, out for exercise, talked to each other under his window in the local *lingua crioula*, but Jeffy understood not a word of it.

Toward the evening of the second day of his confinement, Jeffy was at his usual perch when a wind arose. It blew hotly through the prison, and continued to blow. The heavy cloud was shredded away, revealing the blue of the sky for the first time in days. The chief guard, a swarthy man with immense mustaches, came out into the courtyard, sampled the air, approved, and strolled over to a stone seat under the baobab tree. Dusting it carefully with his handkerchief, he lay down and relaxed.

On top of the wall behind the guard, something moved. A thing like a python uncoiled itself and began to drop down into the courtyard; it seemed to spread over the wall like a stain as it came, but the heavy foliage of the baobab made it difficult to see what was happening. It looked to Jeffy now as if a rubbery curtain set with jewels and starfish were gliding down the wall. Now it landed behind the guard.

Whatever the thing was, it raised a flapper like a snake about to strike and clamped it over the unsuspecting guard's face. Then the rest of its bulk flowed over the man, damping his struggles and covering him like a cloak. Jeffy cried out furiously from his cell, but no one answered, no one cared; most of the staff were down on the waterfront with their girls.

When the thing slid off the chief guard, only a limp and flattened body lay on the bench. The hot wind trifled with its mustaches. The thing grew fingers and expertly removed the ring of keys from the dead man's belt. A segment of it then detached itself from the main bulk, which remained in the shadows as the segment scampered across the yard with the keys. It looked like an animated stool.

"My God!" Jeffy said. "It's coming here."

As he backed away from the window to his cell door, the creature, with one bound, appeared between the bars and dropped the keys into the cell. It jumped in after them.

Bit by bit, more of the thing arrived, dropping down before Jeffy's petrified gaze and finally building into—Gerund, or an intolerable replica of him.

Gerund put out a hand and touched his servant, almost as if he was experimenting.

"It's all right, Jeffy," he said at last, speaking with obvious effort. "You have nothing to fear. No harm will come to you. Take these keys, unlock your cell door, and come with me up to the warden of the prison."

Gray in the face, shaking like a leaf, Jeffy managed to pull himself together enough to obey. The keys rattling in his hand, he tried them one by one in the lock until he found a key that fitted. Like a man mesmerized, he led the way into the corridor, the pseudo-Gerund following closely behind.

No one was about. At one point a guard slept in a tipped-back chair, his heels resting high above his head on the white-washed wall. They did not disturb him. They unlocked the big, barred door at the foot of a private staircase and so ascended into the warden's office. Open doors showed them the way to a balcony overlooking the bay and the central peaks of the island.

On the balcony, alone as usual, drinking wine as usual, a man sat in a wicker chair. He looked small and—yes, alas!—infinitely tired.

"Are you the prison warden?" Gerund asked, stumping into the room.

"I am," I said.

He looked at me for a long while. I could tell then that he was not—what shall I say?—not an ordinary human being. He looked what he was: a forgery of a human being. Even so, I recognized him as Gerund Gyres from the photographs the police had circulated.

"Will you both take a chair?" I asked. "It fatigues me to see you standing."

Neither servant nor master moved.

"Why have you—how have you released your man?" I asked.

"I brought him before you," Gerund said, "so that you may hear what I have to say, and so that you may know that Jeffy is a good servant, has never done me harm. I want him released forthwith."

So, this was a reasonable creature which had compassion. Human or no, it was something I could talk to. So many men with whom I have to deal have neither reason nor compassion.

"I am prepared to listen," I said, pouring myself more wine. "As you see, I have little else to do. Listening can be even pleasanter than talking."

Whereupon Gerund began to tell me everything I have now set down here to the best of my ability. Jeffy and I listened in silence; though the bondman undoubtedly understood little, I grasped quite enough to make my insides turn cold. After all, was not my copy of Pamlira's work on paraevolution lying at my elbow?

In the quiet that fell when Gerund finished, we heard the sunset Angelus ringing out from a Praia steeple; it brought me no anodyne, and the hard, hot wind carried its notes away. I knew already that a darkness was falling that no prayers would lighten.

"So then," I said, finding my voice, "as warden, the first

point I must make is that you, Gerund Gyres, as I must call you, have committed murder: on your own admission, you killed my chief guard."

"That was an error," Gerund said. "You must realize that I —who am a composite of Je Regard, Cyro Gyres and Gerund Gyres, to say nothing of the numerous fish absorbed on my swim up from the subport—I believed I could absorb any human being. It would not be death; we are alive. But your guard defied absorption. So did Jeffy, here, when I touched him."

"Why do you think that is?" I asked stiffly.

He grew a smile on his face. I averted my eyes from it.

"We learn fast," he said. "We cannot absorb humans who are not conscious of themselves as part of the process of nature. If they cling to the outmoded idea of man as a species apart, their cells are antagonistic to ours and absorption will not take place."

"Do you mean to tell me you can only—er—absorb a cultured man?" I asked.

"Exactly. With animals it is different. Their consciousness is only a natural process; they offer us no obstacle."

I believe it was at this point that Jeffy jumped over the balcony rail into the bushes below. He picked himself up unhurt, and we watched his massive frame dwindle from the road as he ran away. Neither of us spoke; I hoped he might go to bring help, but if Gerund thought of that he gave no sign.

"Really, I don't think I understand what you mean at all," I said, playing for time. And I don't think I did grasp it then; to tell you the truth, I was feeling so sick that the whole prison seemed to reel around me. This heavy pseudoman made me more frightened than I knew I could be. Though I fear neither life nor death, before the half-alive I was shivering with the chill of horror.

"I don't understand about absorbing only cultured people," I said, almost at random.

This time it did not bother to open its mouth to answer.

"Culture implies fuller understanding. Today there is culturally speaking only one way to that understanding: through Galingua. I can only liberate the cells of those who are able to use that semantic tool, those whose whole biochemical bondage has already been made malleable by it. The accident that happened to Je Regard releases abilities already latent in every Galingua-speaking person throughout the Galaxy. Here and now on Yinnisfar, a giant step ahead has been taken—unexpected, yet the inevitable climax to the employment of Galingua."

"So then," I said, feeling better as I began to comprehend, "you are the next evolutionary step as predicted by Pamlira in *Paraevolution?*"

"Roughly speaking, yes," he said. "I have the total awareness Pamlira spoke of. Each of my cells has that gift; therefore I am independent of fixed form, that bane of every multicelled creature before me."

I shook my head.

"You seem to me not an advance but a retrogression," I said. "Man is, after all, a complex gene hive; you are saying you can turn into single cells, but single cells are very early forms of life."

"All my cells are *aware*," he said emphatically. "That's the difference. Genes build themselves into cells and cells into the gene hive called man in order to develop *their* potentialities, not man's. The idea of man's being able to develop was purely an anthropomorphic concept. Now the cells have finished with this shape called man; they have exhausted its possibilities and are going on to something else."

To this there seemed nothing to say, so I sat quietly, sipping my drink and watching the shadows grow, spreading from the mountains out to sea. I was still cold but no longer shaking.

"Have you nothing else to ask me?" Gerund inquired, almost with puzzlement in his voice. You hardly expect to hear a monster sound puzzled.

"Yes," I said. "Just one thing. Are you happy?"

The silence, like the shadows, extended itself toward the horizon.

"I mean," I amplified, "if I had a hand in modeling a new species, I'd try and make something more capable of happiness than man. Curious creatures that we are, our best moments come when we are striving for something; when the thing's achieved—la—we are full of unrest again. There is a divine discontent, but divine content comes only to the beasts of the pasture, who regardlessly crop down snails with their grass. The more intelligent a man is, the more open he is to doubt; conversely, the bigger fool he is, the more likely he is to be pleased with his lot. So I'm asking, are you, new species, happy?"

"Yes," Gerund said positively. "As yet I am but three people: Regard, Cyro, Gerund. The last two have struggled for years for full integration—as do all human couples—and now have found it, a fuller integration than was ever feasible before. What humans instinctively seek, we instinctively have; we are the completion of a trend. We can never be anything but happy, no matter how many people we absorb."

Keeping my voice steady, I said, "You'd better start absorbing me then, since that must be what you intend."

"Eventually all human cells will come under the new regime," Gerund said. "But first the word of what is happening must be spread to make people receptive to us, to soften further what Galingua has already softened. Everyone must know, so that we can carry out the absorption process. That is your duty. You are a civilized man, warden; you must write to Pamlira for a start, explaining what has occurred. Pamlira will be interested."

He paused. Three cars swept up the road and turned in at the main gate of the prison. Jeffy, then, had had enough intelligence to go for help.

"Supposing I will not aid you?" I asked. "Why should I hurry man's extinction? Supposing I acquaint the Gal-Fed Council with the truth, and get them to blow this whole island to bits? It would be a simple—get out!—a simple matter—confound it!"

We were suddenly surrounded by butterflies. In impatiently brushing them away, I had knocked over my bottle of wine. The air was full of thousands of butterflies, fluttering around us like paper; the darkening sky was thick with them. The angriest gestures of the hand could not clear them away.

"What is this?" Gerund spluttered. For the first time, I personally saw him out of shape, as he grew another attachment to wave the dainty creatures off. It sprouted from what had been his ear, and flailed the air about his head. I can only say I was nauseated. It cost me the greatest effort to keep a grip on myself.

"As a creature so aware of nature," I said, "you should enjoy this spectacle. These are Painted Lady butterflies, blown in thousands off their migratory tracks. We get them here most years. This hot wind, which we call the marmtan, carries them westward across the ocean from the continent."

Now I could hear people running up the stairs. They would be able to deal suitably with this creature, whose reasonable words were so in contrast to his unreasonable appearance. I continued, speaking more loudly, so that if possible he would be taken unawares. "It's not entirely a misfortune for the butterflies. There are so many of them, no doubt they have eaten most of their food on the mainland and would have starved had they not been carried here by the wind. An admirable example of nature looking after its own."

"Admirable!" he echoed. I could scarcely see him for bright wings. The rescue party was in the next room. They burst out with Jeffy at their head, carrying atomic weapons.

"There he is," I shouted.

But he was not there. Regard-Cyro-Gerund had gone. Taking a tip from the Painted Ladies, he had split into a thousand units, volplaning away on the breeze, safely, invincibly, lost among the crowd of bright insects.

So I come to what is really not the end but the beginning of the story. Already, a decade has passed since the events in the Capverde Islands. What did I do? Well, I did nothing; I neither wrote to Pamlira nor called Gal-Fed Council. With the marvelous adaptability of my species, I managed in a day or two to persuade myself that "Gerund" would never succeed, or that somehow or other he had misinterpreted what was happening to him. And so, year by year, I hear the reports of the human race growing fewer and I think, "Well, anyway, they're happy," and I sit up here on my balcony and drink my wine and let the sea breezes blow on me. In this climate, and at this post, nothing more should be expected of me.

And why should I excite myself for a cause in which I have never believed? When Nature passes a law it cannot be repealed; for her prisoners there is no escape—and we are all her prisoners. So I sit tight and take another drink. There is only one proper way to become extinct: with dignity.

7

THE
MEGALOPOLIS
MILLENNIA

It is ironical that when men could finally have liberated themselves from dependence on the machine with the help of that philo-somatic tool, Galingua, they should have found themselves facing an overwhelming danger for which Galingua itself was responsible.

By no means all of them faced this danger with the weary resignation of the prison warden. Give a man an enemy and you bring out both the best and the worst in him. With its hackles up, humanity went in to fight. Yet it is worth noting that even in this crisis there were many people who took the long view and resigned themselves—not from indifference but for finer reasons—to what they saw as their inevitable fate.

These reasons were set forth cogently enough by Chize Dutremey, writing some five hundred years after Pamlira's time, when a quarter of Yinnisfar's population had faded into individually sentient cells and the whole complex structure of stellar intercourse was disintegrating.

"The Dual Theory, that religion most generally accepted by enlightened men throughout the Galaxy," Chize wrote, "claims that the universe was created by two similar but opposed forces, To and Pla-To. To created nonsentient matter; Pla-To, coming later, created sentient matter. The two forces are hostile to—or at best indifferent to—each other. Pla-To is by far the less powerful, for sentient matter must always depend to some extent upon nonsentient.

"The objectives of the two forces are as opposed as their natures. As far as man can comprehend To at all, his objectives may be described in the word endurance. He must endure through the matter he has created, perpetuating himself as it is perpetuated; and its perpetuation is only challenged by Pla-To.

"The sentient forces of Pla-To are infinitely weaker than his opponent's. For one thing, the very nature of sentience is transient, for sentience entails development, which in its turn entails decay. Sentient objects, moreover, are easily overcome by nonsentient ones: floods, earthquakes, novae. And not only overcome, but totally destroyed—and in that destruction, converted into nonsentient objects.

"Pla-To has only one effective defense against the vast opposed ranks of nullity. The total material in the universe is finite and (eventually) exhaustible; the forces of To cannot therefore increase. But the forces of Pla-To can, for life and sentience are created out of the nonsentient, thus increasing themselves and decreasing the enemy. Man is one of Pla-To's finest instruments, for through him sentience is spread from planet to planet, banishing nullity."

So said Chize Dutremey, in her exposition of the Dual Theory. Put briefly, it may be said that total feeling was to the total good, while the total triumph of To would bring the evil of total nonfeeling. Many men were quick to observe that the evolution of sentient cells was a further, major step toward To's defeat; it represented an increase in feeling: for every small beacon called man, there could now be thousands of thousands of small lights launched against To's darkness.

The Dual Theory was the first galactic religion. From its inception of the hub world of Rolf, it stood as cool and aloof from men as a tall mountain and as distant from their affairs as a Plutonian Hill. It recognized life and the finish of life; it recognized the chill of the night and the length of its ultimate duration; it recognized the shortness of day and its beauty. It knew that beyond all joy lay a curtain of something too cruel to be called sorrow, too noble to be called misery; that all flesh was air, breathed and finished in a minute—but that in that minute, in that time for doing, lay all the truth that was. It was a galactic religion, hard to grasp and uncomforting when grasped, for which very reason the true adults of those days turned to it. It offered them no afterglow beyond the grave, nor did it speak of golden voices from other spheres; it bestowed no rewards for virtue or punishments for weakness. It had no altars. No one decked its shrines with flowers; no one set its tenets to a trumpeting music. Yet their hearts took on strength and depth from its sober truth.

The believers were accordingly not afraid to demonstrate that the Dual Theory set little store by man and his glories. Man was an incidental in Pla-To's path to full sentience. The prime sentient unit was the cell. Now that it had learned to be itself by itself, it was forsaking that grouping called man to which it had so long adhered, just as man had long since abandoned the tribe structure necessary to his primitive days. Therefore believers could not, had no right to, oppose a step which according to their faith furthered the aims of Pla-To.

All of which, for many men, smacked of stupidity and suicide. Whatever theories they held or did not hold, in practice they believed in the survival of man—and, more particularly, of themselves.

The use of Galingua was prohibited. This meant the severing of those close bonds with which the planetary concourse had joined itself. Even the Self-perpetuating War lost impetus, ceasing entirely in many regions. Although the old "solid" system of space travel by spaceship was slowly reintroduced, the Galaxy—even like man himself—began disintegrating into its individual members.

War against the conqueror cell was on. Mainly it had to be a defensive battle. At the same time religious strife broke out, nonbelievers fighting the Theorists who, as we have seen, were bound to oppose those they regarded as unwitting agents of To.

Eventually the believers were massacred almost to a man. The legions which overcame them, driven by fear, gave no quarter; clothed in fantastic antibiotic armors which lent them some protection against vagabond cells, they filled their already threatened worlds with death.

On Yinnisfar, the strife was particularly bitter, dying down only when the menace of the cells itself became no longer a vital issue.

Many ways of combating this menace were introduced, but the most effective were the aerostomas. The aerostomas represented a compromise between To and Pla-To. They were semisentient flying things made of Pyrocathus 12, a malleable material susceptible to human thought impulses. Little more than airborne stomachs, the aerostomas flew low over land and sea on every planet threatened with cellular disintegration, swallowing the vagabond cells, compressing and stifling them. Of noncellular origin, the aerostomas were immune to disintegration.

A new princely order arose on Yinnisfar, the Triumphing Men, who went forth like knights to battle with the in-

visible foe, aerostomas perching on their shoulders or circling restlessly in the air above.

Hard the Triumphing Men were, hard and brave. In the millennia that followed, they became a legend, and the legend was embodied in Thraldemener. Thraldemener's exploits were many and his victories frequent, although there seems little doubt that his deeds have gained in the retelling.

Whether humanity would ever have succeeded in vanquishing a foe which swelled its ranks from humanity is debatable. A rapid form of cancer destroyed the cells. In their struggle for survival, they had overreached themselves. Virtually a new form of life, they were unstable, and their instability was their undoing. When diseased matter was first incorporated into their ranks, they had no way of combating it. The cancerous cells were a ravening enemy in their midst, maiming, destroying, obliterating. Man awoke one day to find himself again master of his worlds, with only a thin ash in the meadows to mark the end of one of nature's strangest experiments.

This is no place to describe in detail the reconstruction of a federated Galaxy, which man undertook in a mood compounded at once of savagery and despair. It took more than a million years, for something of his old thrust had gone. He had learned a new lesson: that he could be superseded from within, that even in his keenest hour of triumph those cosmic chess players, To and Pla-To, regarded him simply as a seedbed for future experiment. The Federation was patched; its old easy confidence lay beyond mending.

Yinnisfar, under the Galingua regime for a far shorter period than most of its sister planets, had solid spaceships still in commission. With these, it was able to take a lead in galactic trade. The spirit of its people, hardened under the regime of the Triumphing Men, rendered it fit to compete with the most mercenary of rivals.

Its banks swelled like overfed bellies. Its merchants walked in golden slippers. The city of Nunion sprawled and lost its shape like a gorged python. Mammon was back on his throne, and the following fragment reflects only a tiny portion of his face.

THE MIGHTY CREATURE WAS REELING. THE HUNTER'S LAST shot had caught it right between its eyes. Now, all fifty graceful tons of it, the beast reared up high above the treetops, trumpeting in agony. For a moment the sun, beautiful and baleful, caught it poised like an immense swan, before it fell

—silent now, no more protesting—headlong into the undergrowth.

"And there lies another triumph for Man the Unconquerable," proclaimed the commentator. "On this planet, as on others, all life finally bows before a man from Yinnisfar. Yes, every one of these monsters will be slaughtered by the time—"

By this time someone had warned the projectionist of the new arrival now waiting to use the little editing theater, and the projectionist, in a panic, cut everything. The 3-D image vanished, the sound slicked out. Lights came on, revealing Big Cello of Supernova Solids standing by the entrance.

"Hope we didn't disturb you," Big Cello said, watching everyone hustling up to leave.

"Not at all, Cello 69," a subdirector replied. "We'll solidify this one tomorrow."

"I wouldn't like to think we'd interrupted," Big Cello said blandly. "But Rhapsody 182 here has something he seems to want to show us." And he nodded, not without easy menace, at the lean figure of Harsch-Benlin, known to the inmates of Supernova as Rhapsody 182.

Two minutes later, the last minion had fled from the theater, leaving the intruding party in occupation.

"Well, Rhapsody, let's see what you have to show us," Big Cello observed heavily, settling his bulk in one of the armchair seats.

"Sure thing, B. C.," Harsch-Benlin said. He was one of the few men on the Supernova lot allowed to call the chief by initials, rather than by the full United name. He jumped now, with a parody of athleticism, onto the narrow stage in front of the solidscreen and smiled down at his audience. It consisted of some twenty-five people, half of whom Rhapsody knew only by sight. The company broke down roughly into four groups: the chief and his orgmen; Rhapsody's own orgmen, headed by Ormolu 3; a handful from Story and Market Response with their orgmen; plus the usual quota of attractive stylus recorders.

"The idea's imbedded in a solid," Rhapsody began, "that's going to give Supernova a terrific boost, because it's going to have our studios as background, and some of our personnel as players. At the same time, it's going to pack colossal punch in terms of human drama and audience appeal. Not only that—it's backdrop is Nunion, the greatest planetary capital in the Galaxy."

Rhapsody paused for effect. Several members of his audience were lighting up aphrohales. All were quiet.

"I can see you're asking yourselves," Rhapsody said, essaying a smile, "just how I intend to cram so much meat into one two-hour solid. I'll show you."

He raised a hand eloquently, as a signal to his projectionist. A solid appeared on the screen.

It was the face of a man. A man in his late forties. The years that had dried away the flesh had only succeeded in revealing, under the fine skin, the nobility of bone structure: the tall forehead, the set of cheekbone, the justness of the jaw. He was talking, although the sound was off, leaving the animation of the features to speak for themselves. The countenance completely dwarfed Rhapsody 182.

"This, ladies and gentlemen," Rhapsody said, clenching his fists and holding them out before him, "is the face of Ars Staykr."

The audience began sitting up, looking at one another, gauging the climate of opinion. Rhapsody had deliberately called Staykr by his true rather than his United name. It was customary in big combines like Supernova to use people's district plus block number as names. Not only did this serve to present a united front to confuse outsiders; it helped insiders to place you financially, for districts in Nunion were islands divided according to grandeur. You had to be a credit king to live on Cello, whereas on Pelt and Trickle no one but deadbeats were permitted to live.

Ars Staykr had been an individualist. Somehow, his United name of Bastion 44 had never fitted, as Rhapsody now emphasized. Gratified at the audience's response, he continued.

"The face of a great man. Ars Staykr! A genius known only to a narrow circle of men, here in this very studio where he worked; yet all who knew him admired and—why don't I say it?—*loved* him. I had the honor to be his right-hand man back in the days when he was boss of Documentary Two. I plan this solid to be his biography—a tribute to Ars Staykr, Bastion 44."

He paused. If he could swing this one on Big Cello and Company he was made, because if it boosted Ars Staykr it was also going to boost Harsch-Benlin until that erstwhile Rhapsody ended up mellow on the Cello levels.

"Staykr ended up in the gutter!" someone called out. That was Starfield 1337, a troublemaker.

"I am glad someone raised that point," Rhapsody continued, carefully snubbing Starfield by omitting his name. "Staykr finished up in the gutter. He couldn't make the grade. This solid is going to show why. It's going to show just how much grit is needed simply to stay sane in Nunion. It's going to show how much grit is needed to serve the public as *we* serve them—because, like I said, it's going to be a solid not just about Ars Staykr, but about Supernova, and about Nunion, and about Life. In short, it's going to have everything."

The gentle face faded from the screen, leaving the small figure of Rhapsody standing on the platform alone. Although thin to the point of emaciation, Rhapsody perpetually consumed slimming tablets for the luxury of hearing his underlings refer to him as "gangling," which he held to be a term of affection.

"And the beauty of this solid is," he continued dramatically, "the beauty's that it's already half-made! Written, directed, solidified."

Images began to grow in the seemingly limitless depths of the cube. Something as intricate and lovely as the magnification of a snowflake stirred and seemed to drift toward the audience. It enlarged, sprouting detail, elaborating itself, until every tiny branch had other branches. It seemed, thanks to clever camera work, to be an organic growth; then the descending, slowing viewpoint at length revealed it to be a creation of concrete and imperve and ferroline, molded by man into buildings and thoroughfares, into levels and mazes, stabbing into the air or burrowing into the earth.

"This," Rhapsody pronounced, "is the fabulous city—*our* fabulous city—the city of Nunion. Nunion—jelled by Unit Two under Staykr at the height of his powers, twenty years ago. This solid was to be his greatest work; it was never completed, for reasons I will tell you later. But the sixteen reels of unedited cathusjell he left behind as his greatest memorial have lain in our vaults all that time. I dug them out the other day.

"Now I'm not going to talk for a while. I'm going to ask you to sit back and appreciate the sheer beauty of these shots. I'm going to ask you to try and judge their value in terms of aesthetic reaction and viewer appeal. I'm going to ask you to relax and watch a masterpiece, in which I'm proud to say I had something of a hand."

The image continued to sink gradually, below the highest towers, through the aerial levels, the pedestrian (human and ahuman) esplanades, the various transport and service strata, down to the ground, the imperve pavement, at which point a convex glass traffic guide reflected in miniature the whole of that long camera descent from the skies. Then the focus shifted laterally, taking in the vermilion boots of a Flux officer.

Almost unnoticed, a commentary had begun. It was a typical Unit Two commentary: quiet, unemphatic, spoken in Ars Staykr's own voice.

"On the seventy thousand planets which occupy the single Galaxy inhabited by man, there is no more vast or diverse city than Nunion," the commentary said. "It has become a fable to all men of all races. To describe it is impossible without descending into statistics and figures, and this is to lose sight of the reality; we ask you to explore some of the reality with us. Forget the facts and figures: look instead at the flux-ways and mansions and, above all, at the individuals which comprise Nunion. Look, and ask yourself: How does one find the heart of a great city? What secret lies at the core of it when one arrives?"

Nunion had grown over the ten islands of an archipelago in the temperate zone of Yinnisfar, spreading from the nearby continent. Five hundred bridges, a hundred and fifty sub-fluxes, sixty heliplane routes, and innumerable ferries, gondolas and sailing craft interconnected the eleven sectors and forty-five districts. Lining the water lanes or breaking the seemingly endless phalanxes of streets went avenues of either natural or polycathic trees, with here and there—perhaps at some focal point like the Ishrail Memorial—the rare and lovely jenny-merit, newly imported, perpetually flowering. The camera swept over Clive Amethyst Bridge now, hovering before the first block beyond the waterway. A young man was coming out of the block, springing down the outer steps three at a time. On his face were mingled excitement, triumph and joy. He could hardly contain himself. Buoyed with exultation, he could not walk fast enough. He was the young man in any large city: the man about to make his mark, to score his first success, confident beyond sense, exuberant beyond measure. In him one could see the drive that had reached out to seventy thousand planets and dreamed of seventy thousand more.

The commentator did not say this. The picture said it for him, catching the young man's strut, his angular shadow sharp and restless on the pavement. Sharp and restless, too, the scene changed, angular shadows becoming angular shapes. Down billions of miles of pipe that were Nunion's veins and drains swam the changing ghost shapes of pseudo-leucocytes. With eerie mobility, they preyed on the sewage of the megapolis, ingesting it, cleaning it. Sealed away from human sight, the half-live phantoms went about their needs, which also served the city's.

Others of the capital's servitors paraded through the illusory emptiness of the cube: The ahuman menials whose immunity to hard radiation had earned them the task of tending the universal air-conditioning. The mechanical brains out at Starfield. The human-brain culture under Peach Bosphorus that handled a guaranteed two billion decisions every day. The Undead of the Communications Exchanges, where pepped nerves routed with mindless precision the messages of every district.

The pictures were brilliant, at once clear but nonliteral. No commentary was used, for none was needed. But Rhapsody 182 could not stay silent. He came forward so that his figure bit its silhouette out of the solid.

"That's the way it was with Staykr," he said. "Always digging for what he called 'the exact, revealing detail.' Maybe that's why he got no farther than he did; he drove us crazy for the sake of that detail."

"These are just shots of a big city," a man from Story called up impatiently. "We've seen this sort of cubage before, Harsch. Just what does it all add up to?"

"Use your eyes. See the pattern forming," Harsch replied. "That was how it was where Staykr was concerned; he let the thing evolve, without imposing a pattern. Watch this coming shot now for gentle comedy. . . ."

Young lovers had come sweeping up a Bastion water lane in a powered float. They moored, stepped ashore, and walked arm in arm across a mosaic walk to the nearest café. They chatted animatedly as they found a table. Background music changed tempo; the focus of attention slid from the lovers to the waiters. Their smoothness of manner while serving was contrasted with their indifference when they were behind scenes, in the squalor and confusion of the kitchens. A waiter was followed off duty down to subterranean Pelt, where he submerged himself in a two-credit tub of dyraco and slept.

"Get the idea?" Rhapsody asked his audience. "Ars Staykr is digging. He's peeling off stratum after stratum of the mightiest city of all time. Before we're through, you're going to see just what he found at the bottom."

Hardly for a moment had he taken his eyes off Big Cello, whose deadpan countenance was partially hidden by wreaths of aphrohale. The chief now crossed his legs; that could be bad, a sign perhaps of impatience. Rhapsody, who had learned to be sensitive about such things, thought it time to try a direct sounding. Coming to the edge of the stage, he leaned forward and said ingratiatingly, "Can you see it building, B. C.?"

"I'm still sitting here," Big Cello answered. It could be called a relatively enthusiastic response.

"Those of you who never had the privilege of meeting Ars," Rhapsody continued, "will be asking, 'What sort of man could reveal a city with such genius?' Not to keep you in suspense any longer, I'll tell you. When Ars was on this last assignment, I was just a youngster in the solid business. I learned a lot from him, in the matter of plain, everyday humanity as well as in technique. We're going to show you a bit of film now that a cameraman of Unit Two took of Ars without his knowing. I believe you'll find it—sort of moving."

The solid was suddenly there, seeming to fill all the audience's vision. In a corner of one of Nunion's many starports, Ars Staykr and several of his documentary team sat against junked oxygenation equipment, taking lunch. Ars was sixty-eight and passing his middle years. Hair blown over his eyes, he could be seen devouring a gigantic kyfeff sandwich and talking to a youth with a space cut. Looking around at the solid, Rhapsody identified his younger self with some embarrassment and said, "You have to remember this was taken all of twenty years back."

"You weren't so gangling in those days," one of the audience called.

Ars Staykr was speaking. "Cello 69 has given us the chance to go through with this," he was saying. "So let's see we use the chance properly. Anyone in a city this size can pick up interesting faces, or build up architectural angles into a pattern with the help of a background noise. Let's try for something deeper. What I want to find is what really lies at the heart of the greatest metropolis ever known to man."

"Supposing there is no heart, Staykr?" the youthful Rhapsody asked. (He had been only a Tiger dweller in those days.) "I mean—you hear of heartless men and women; couldn't this simply be a heartless city?"

"A semantic quibble," Ars Staykr replied. "All men and women have hearts, even the cruel ones. Same with cities. I'm not denying Nunion isn't a cruel city in many ways. People who live in it have to fight continually. The good in them gradually gets overlaid and lost. You start good, you end bad just because you—oh, hell—you forget, I suppose. You forget you're human."

Ars Staykr paused and looked searchingly at the blank young face before him. "Never mind watching out for Nunion," he said, almost curtly. "Watch out for yourself."

He stood up, wiping his big hands on his slacks. One of his compo crew offered him an aphrohale and said, "Well, that's it on the starport angle, Staykr; we've jelled all we need to here. What sector do we head for next?"

Ars Staykr looked around smilingly, the set of his jaw noticeable. "We take on the politicians next," he said.

The youthful Rhapsody scrambled to his feet, his manner noticeably more aggressive.

"Say, if we could clear up the legal rackets of Nunion," he said, "why, we'd get our solids and be doing everyone a favor, too. We'd be famous, all of us!"

"I was just a crazy, idealistic kid back in those days," the mature Rhapsody, at once abashed and delighted, protested to the audience. "I'd still to learn that life is nothing but a kind of co-ordination of rackets." He smiled widely to indicate that he might be kidding, saw that Big Cello was not smiling, and lapsed into silence.

In the cube, Unit Two was picking up its traps. The cumbersome polyhedron of a trans-Burst freighter from far Lapraca sank into the landing pits behind them and blew piercingly.

"I'll tell you the sort of thing we want to try and capture," Ars Staykr told his team as he shouldered a pack of equipment. "When I first came to this city to join Supernova, I was standing in the lobby of the Justice Building before an important industrial case was being tried. A group of local politicians about to give evidence passed me, and I heard one say as they went in—I've never forgotten it—'Have your hatreds ready, gentlemen.' For me, it will always symbolize the way that prejudice can engulf a man. Touches like that we must have."

Ars Staykr and Unit Two trudged out of the picture, shabby, determined. The solid faded, and there before the screen stood Rhapsody 182, spruce, determined.

"It still doesn't begin to stack up, Rhap," a voice spoke up. It was Rhapsody Double Seven, a rival of Rhapsody's, and Big Cello's personnel manager. You had to be careful with a man like that.

"Perhaps you missed the subtleties," Rhapsody suggested instantly. "The thing's stacking fine. That little cameo has just demonstrated to you why Ars never made the grade. He talked too much. He shot off his mouth to kids like I was then. He wasn't hard. He was nothing more or less than just an artist. Right?"

"If you say so, Rhap," the answer came levelly, but Double Seven turned at once to say something inaudible to Big Cello.

Rhapsody made a brusque signal to the projection box. He would swing this deal on Supernova if he had to stay here all afternoon and evening to do it.

Behind him, Ars Staykr's Nunion was re-created once more, a city which administered the might of Yinnisfar's growing dominance and magnetized the wealth of a galaxy, assembled as the mind of Ars Staykr had visualized it two decades before.

Evening was falling over its maze of ferroline canyons. The sun set; great globes of atomic light tethered in the sky poured their radiance over thoroughfares moving with a new awareness. The original commentary dimmed, giving Rhapsody the opportunity to provide his own.

"Night," he said briskly. "Ars caught it all as it's never been caught before or since. He used to tell me, I remember, that night was the time a city showed its claws. We spent two weeks looking for sharp, broken shadows. The craze for significant detail again."

The clawed shadows moved in, fangs of light etched against the dark flanks of side alleys. An almost tangible restlessness, like the noisy silence of a jungle, moved across the ramps and squares of Nunion; even the present onlookers could feel it. They sat more alertly in their seats.

Behind a façade of civilization, the night life of Nunion had a primitive ferocity; the Jurassic wore evening dress. In Ars Staykr's interpretation it was essentially a dreary world, the amalgam of the homesicknesses and lusts of the many thousand nations that had drifted to Yinnisfar. The individual was lost in an atom-lit wilderness where ninety million people could be alone together within a few square farlings.

It was quite clear that the thronging multitudes, waiting in line for leg shows and jikey joints, were harmless. Living in flocks, they had developed the flock mentality. They were too harmless to tear anything of value out of the matter of Nunion; all they seemed to ask for was a good time.

Into the cube came the hard-steppers—the ones who could afford to buy solitude and a woman or pneuma-dancer to go with it. They drifted above the sparkling avenues in bubbles; they ate in undersea restaurants, nodding in brotherly fashion to sharks swimming beyond glass walls; they wined in a hundred dives; they sat absorbed over games of chance. Always, at the imperious signal of an eye, there was someone to come running, a man who sweated and trembled as he ran. In short, a galactic city; power must remember it is powerful.

The scene changed. The view swept over the Old Jandanagger and began to investigate Bosphorus Concourse.

The Concourse lay at the heart of Nunion. Here the search for pleasure reached its peak. Barkers cried rival attractions, polyhermaphros signaled, liquor flowed in never-ending streams, cinema vied with participation hall, quirps and quaints beckoned from drifting floats, women of the night moved sleek and busy, a thousand sensations—the perversions of a galaxy—were available at a price. Man, conscious as never before of all of his cells, had invented a different thrill for each.

Rhapsody 182 could not resist adding a word.

"Have you ever seen such realism?" he demanded. "Ordinary folks—folks like you, like me—getting down to having themselves a time. Think what promotion these shots are for Nunion! And where've they been these last twenty years? Why, down in our vaults, neglected, almost lost. Nobody would ever have seen them if I hadn't hunted them up!"

Big Cello spoke.

"I've seen them, Rhapsody," he said throatily. "They're just too sordid to have popular appeal."

Rhapsody stood absolutely still. A dark stain rose in his face. Those few words told him—and everyone else present—exactly where he stood. If he persisted, he would rouse the chief's anger; if he backed down, he would lose face.

In the solid behind Rhapsody, men and women jostled for admission to an all-sense horror show, *Death in Death Cell Six*. Above them, gigantic, was a quasi-live jell of a man being choked, head down, eyes popping, mouth agape.

"We needn't show all this sordid stuff, of course," Rhapsody said, grinning as if in pain. "I'm just giving it a runover to put the general idea before you. We'll settle on the final details later, naturally." Naturally.

Big Cello nodded. "You're too sold on Bastion 44, though, Rhap," he said kindly. "He was only a bum with a camera, after all."

Ars Staykr's city was emptying now. Crumpled aphrohale packets, minni-newscasts, tickets, programs, preventos, sick-sticks, handbills, and flowers lay in the gutter. The revelers were straggling home to sleep.

A fog settled lightly over Bosphorus Concourse, emphasizing the growing vacancy of the place. A fat man, clothes unbuttoned, reeled out of a participation hall and made for the nearest moveway. It spun him off like a leaf in a drain.

Three and one half sounded from Pla-To Court. Lights snapped off in a deserted restaurant, leaving on the retina an afterimage of upturned chairs. Even the Cello pleasure domes went dim. One last drab clattered wearily home, clutching her handbag tightly.

Yet the Concourse was not empty of humanity. The remorseless eye of the camera hunted down, in sundry doorways, the last watchers of the scene—the ones who had stood, motionless, not participating, when the evening was at its height. Watching the crowd, they waited in doorways as if peering from warrens. From the shadows, their faces gleamed with a terrible, inexpressible tension. Only their eyes moved.

"These men," Rhapsody said, "really fascinated Ars Staykr. They were his discovery. He believed that if anyone could lead him to the heart of the city, these people could, these subterraneans in doorways. Night after night they were there. Staykr called them 'the impotent specters of the feast.' "

The solidscreen blanked, then filled with form once again. An overhead camera tracked two men down a canal-side walk. Ars Staykr and his young assistant, Rhapsody 182. They had movewayed down to the quiet side of Tiger.

The two figures paused outside a shabby boutique, looking doubtfully at the sign, A. WILLITTS, COSTUMES AND VESTMENTS.

"I have the feeling we're going to turn up something," Ars was saying as the sound came on. "We're going to hear what a city really is, from someone who must have felt its atmosphere most keenly. With this fellow, we're digging right down into the heart of it. But it won't be pleasant."

Darkness. It seemed to seep out of the black G-suits; they were the antique tailor's specialty, hanging stiff and bulky around the walls, funereal in the gloom. The costumier, Willitts, was a newt of a man; his features were recognizable as those of one of the Concourse night watchers, now trailed to his lair.

Willitt's eyes bulged and glistened like those of a drowning rat. He denied ever going to Bosphorus Concourse. When Ars persisted, he fell silent, dangling his little fingers against the counter.

"I'm not a flux officer," Ars Staykr said. "I'm simply curious. I want to know why you stand there every night the way you do."

"It's nothing to be ashamed of," Willitts muttered, dropping his eyes. "I don't do anything."

"That's just it. You don't do anything. Why do you—and others like you—stand there not doing anything? What are you thinking of? What do you see? What do you feel?"

"I've got business to attend to," Willitts protested. "I'm busy. Can't you see I'm busy?"

"I want to know what you feel, how you tick, Willitts."

"Leave me alone, will you?"

"Answer my questions and I'll go away."

"We could make it worth your while, Willitts," young Rhapsody added, with a knowing look.

The little man's eyes were furtive. He licked his lips. He seemed so tired, his tiny frame devoid of blood.

"Leave me alone," he said. "That's all I ask—leave me alone. I'm not hurting you, am I? A customer might come in any time. I'm not answering your questions. Now please get out of here."

Unexpectedly, Ars Staykr jumped, pinning the little man backward across the counter. Of the two, Staykr's face was the more desperate.

"Willitts," he said, "I've got to know. I've *got* to know. I've been digging into this cesspit of a city week after week, and you're the thing I've found at the bottom of it. You're going to tell me what it feels like down there or, so help me, I'll break your neck."

"How can I tell you?" Willitts demanded with sudden, mouselike fury. "I can't tell you. I can't. I haven't got the words. You'd have to be me—or my kind—before you'd understand."

In the end they gave it up and left Willitts panting, lying behind his counter in the dust.

"I didn't mean to lose control," Ars Staykr said, pressing

his brow, licking his knuckles, as he emerged from the shop. He must have known the camera was on him, but was too preoccupied to care. "Something just went blank inside me. We've all got our hatreds far too ready, I guess. But I must find out. . . ."

His set face loomed larger and larger in the cube, eclipsing all else. One eyelid was flickering uncontrollably. He moved out of sight.

Everyone was talking in the audience now, except the chief; they had all enjoyed the beating up.

"Seriously," Ormolu 3 was saying, "that last scene had something. You'd resolidify, of course, with proper actors, have a few broken teeth. Maybe finish with the little guy getting knocked into the canal."

Timing his exits was a specialty with Rhapsody. He had them awake and now he'd show them no more. He came slowly down the few steps into the auditorium.

"So there's the story of a man called Ars Staykr," he said, as his right foot left the last step. "He couldn't take it. After he beat up that little tailor, he dropped everything and disappeared into the stews of Nunion. He didn't even stay to round off his picture, and Unit Two folded then and there. He was a quitter."

"How come we've had to wait twenty years to hear all this?" came a shout from Rhapsody Double Seven.

Carefully, Rhapsody 182 spread his hands wide and smiled.

"Because Ars Staykr was a dirty word when he first quit," he said, aiming his voice at Big Cello, "and after that he was forgotten. Then, well, it happened I ran into Staykr a couple of days back, and that gave me the idea of working over the old Unit Two files."

He tried to move in front of Big Cello, to make it easier for the chief to compliment him on his sagacity if he felt so inclined.

"You mean Ars is still alive?" Double Seven persisted. "He must be quite an old man now. What's he doing, for To's sake?"

"He's a down-and-out, a bum," Rhapsody said. "I didn't care to be seen talking to him, so I got away from him as soon as possible."

He now stood before the chief.

"Well, B. C.," he said, as calmly as he could, "don't tell

me you don't smell a solid there—something to sweep 'em off their feet and knock 'em into the aisles."

As if deliberately prolonging the suspense, Big Cello took another drag on this aphrohale, then removed it gently from his mouth.

"We'd have to have a pair of young lovers in it," Big Cello said.

"Sure," Rhapsody exclaimed, scowling to hide his elation. "Young lovers! There's an idea! A great idea!"

"I see it as a saga of the common man," Hurricane 304 suggested. "We could call it *Our Fair City*—if that title isn't legally sequestered."

"It's a vehicle for Edru Expusso!" someone else suggested.

They were playing with it. Harsch had won the day.

He was hustling out of the little theater when a hand touched his arm and Rhapsody Double Seven pulled him back.

"How did you happen to find Ars Staykr again?" he asked.

"Well," Rhapsody said happily, "I happened to have a rendezvous a couple of nights back. I was looking for a helibubble afterward when I happened to walk through Bosphorus Concourse. This old wreck hanging about in a doorway recognized me and called out."

"It was Ars?"

"It was Ars. I kept on going, of course. But it put me onto the concept of this solid."

"Didn't you ask Ars if he'd found out what was at the heart of the city? That was what he'd gone looking for, wasn't it?"

"What's it matter? That quaint had nothing we'd want to buy. His clothes were in rags, I tell you; why, the crazy fool was shivering with virol I was lucky that bubble came when it did!"

They made the solid—one of Supernova's big-budget productions for the year. It took in credits on every inhabited planet of the Federation, and Rhapsody 182 was a powerful, respected man thereafter. They called it *Song of a Mighty City*; it had three electronic orchestras, seventeen hit tunes and a regiment of pneuma-dancing girls. The solidization was jelled in the studios using the pastel shades deemed most appropriate, and they finally selected a more suitable city than Nunion for backgrounds. Ars Staykr, of course, did not come into it at all.

8

THE
ULTIMATE
MILLENNIA

Again we must use the symbol: Time passed. Time is stretched to its limits, extended almost beyond meaning, for Time now rolls down a gentle decline of innumerable centuries toward the sunset of Yinnisfar and its Galaxy.

It was a time of contrast. Those planets and systems which, while the Self-perpetuating War was in full spate, had once been linked by the bond of enmity had now not enough in common even to be rivals. It was a time of discovery and consolidation; of experiment and abdication; of hope and resignation; of the historian and the prophet. It was a time of the exploration of the inner resources of man; with his last frontiers tamed, man turned in toward the self. There he went on foot, alone, without that gray steed Science in which he had trusted for so long, alone into the labyrinth of his own devices.

Humanity had multiplied. Every world bore a mighty crowd of people, but the crowd no longer jostled and shouted. Each individual remained by choice to himself, an island. It was the silver period of the Age of Splendor and Starlight. Soon only the starlight would remain.

Toward the end of a great pageant, it may be, the stage is at its most crowded; a sea of faces, brightly lit, greets us even as the curtains begin their final downward sweep. Toward the end of a symphony, it may be, the whole orchestra puts forth its full efforts only a minute before silence falls and the music becomes a memory.

Throughout one vast arena, silence was falling, the last silence of all.

I

YOU NEVER KNEW THE BEGINNING OF THAT TRAIN OF EVENTS which led you to Yinnisfar and a world of shadows.

You never knew Shouter by name. He operated far from

what most men reckoned as civilization, right out on the rim of the Galaxy, so that on his frequent sweeps from one planet to another he rarely saw stars on both sides of his cabin. There they would be, a whole galaxyful on one side, burning bright and high, and, on the other—a cliff of emptiness that stretched from eternity to eternity, the distant island universes only accentuating the gulf.

Shouter generally kept his eyes on the stars.

But not on this trip. Shouter was a spool-seller by trade; his little star craft was packed with rack upon rack of microspools. He stocked all kinds, new and antiquarian; philosophical, sociological, mathematical; if you went through them systematically, you could almost piece together the eon-old history of the Galaxy. It was not, however, on these learned spools that Shouter made his best money; they paid for the fuel, but not the drinks. The spools that really brought in the profits dealt with a subject older than history, and with figures more ineluctable than any in the mathematician's vocabulary; their subject was Desire. Erotic spools depicting the devices of lust formed Shouter's stock in trade; and because such items were illegal, Shouter stood in perpetual fear of the customs officials of a hundred worlds.

Now he was elated. He had just neatly outwitted the petty guardians of morality and sold about half his holdings under their very eyes.

That he took too much drink in celebration was to influence your entire life. An empty merrit bottle rolled by his feet. It was hot in the small cabin of his ship, and he dozed off, sprawling over the controls. . . .

Shouter woke muzzily. He sensed something was wrong and his head cleared at once as he peered anxiously into the forward vision tanks. No clouds of accustomed stars were in view. Hurriedly, he flipped on rear vision: there lay the Galaxy like a tinsel disc—far behind him. Shouter swallowed, and checked fuel. Low, but enough to get back on. Fuel, however, was in better supply than air. His oxygen tanks had not been replenished in the hurry of his last departure. He would never get back to the Galaxy alive on the thimbleful that remained.

With an abyss opening in his stomach, Shouter turned to the forward ports again to examine an object he had previously ignored. Apart from the distant phantoms of other galaxies, it was the only object to relieve the inane ubiquity of vacuum—and it was showing a disc. He checked with his instruments. Undoubtedly, it was a small sun.

It puzzled Shouter. His astronomical knowledge was negligible, but he knew that according to the laws there was nothing between galaxies; that long funnel of night shut off galaxy from galaxy as surely as the living were cut off from the dead. He could only suppose this sun ahead to be a tramp star; such things were known, but they naturally roved inside the giant lens of the home Galaxy, in conformity with its gravitational pull. Shouter threw the problem aside unsolved. All that vitally concerned him was whether the sun—wherever it came from—had one or more oxygen planets in attendance.

It had. The sun was a white dwarf with one planet almost as big as itself. A quick stratospheric test as Shouter glided into breaking orbit showed a breathable nitrogen-oxygen balance. Blessing his luck, the spool-seller sped down and landed. A valley fringed by hills and woods embraced him.

He walked out of the airlock in good fettle, leaving the compressor-analyzer systems working to insure full tanks of purified oxygen drawn from the planet's air.

It was hot outside. Shouter had an immediate impression of newness everywhere. Everything seemed fresh, gleaming. His eyes ached at the vividness.

The shores of a lake lay a few yards away. He began to walk toward it, conscious at the same time of a vague discomfort in his breathing. With deliberate effort, he inhaled more slowly, thinking the air might be too rich for him.

Something rose to the surface of the lake a distance away. It looked like a man's head, but Shouter could not be sure; a mist rising from the surface of the lake, as if the waters were hot, obscured detail.

The hurt in his lungs became more definite. He was conscious, too, of a smart spreading across his limbs, almost as if the air were too harsh for them. In his eyes, all things acquired a fluttering spectrum. He had had the assurance of his instruments that all was well, but suddenly that assurance meant nothing: he was in pain.

All in a panic, Shouter turned to get back to his ship. He coughed and fell, dizziness overcoming him. Now he saw it was indeed a man in the misty lake. He shouted for help once only.

You looked across at him, and at once started to swim in his direction.

But Shouter was dying. His cry brought blood up into his throat, splashing out over one hand. He choked, attempting to rise again. You climbed naked out of the lake toward him. He saw you, turning his head heavily, and flung one arm out gesturing toward the ship with its imagined safety. As you got to him, he died.

For a while you knelt by him, considering. Then you turned away and regarded the small starship for the first time. You went over to it, your eyes full of wonder.

The sun rose and set twenty-five times before you mastered all that Shouter's ship contained. You touched everything gently, almost reverently. Those microspools meant little individually to you at first, but you were able to refer back to them and piece the jigsaw of their secrets together, until the picture they gave you formed a whole picture. Shouter's projector was almost worn out before you finished. Then you investigated the ship itself, sucking out its meaning like a thirsty man.

Your thoughts must have moved strangely in those twenty-five days, like sluice gates opening for the first time, as you became yourself.

All you learned then was already knowledge; the way in which you pieced it together was genius, but nevertheless it was knowledge already held by many men, the results of research and experience. Only afterward, when you integrated that knowledge, did you make a deduction on your own behalf. The deduction, involving as it did all the myriad lives in the Galaxy, was so awing, so overwhelming, that you tried to evade it.

You could not; it was inescapable. One clinching fact was the death of Shouter; you knew why he had died. So you had to act, obeying your first moral imperative.

Just for a moment, you looked at your bright world. You would return to it when duty had been done. You climbed up into Shouter's ship, punched out a course on the computer, and headed toward the Galaxy.

2

You came unarmed into the warring city. Your ship lay abandoned on a hill some miles away. You walked as if among the properties of a dream, carrying your own sup-

plies, and demanded to see the leader of the rebel army.
They put innumerable difficulties in your way, but eventually you stood before him because none could gainsay you.

The rebel leader was a hard man with an eye missing,
and he was busy when you entered. He stared at you with
deep mistrust through that single eye; the guards behind him
stroked their fusers.

"I'll give you three minutes," One Eye said.

"I don't want your time," you said easily. "I have plenty
of my own. I also have a plan bigger than any plan of yours.
Do you wish me to show you how to subjugate the Region of
Yinnisfar?"

Now One Eye looked at you again. He saw—how should
it be said?—he saw you were not as other men, that you
were vivider than they. But the Region of Yinnisfar lay
long light years away, impregnable, in the heart of the
Galaxy; for twice ten million years its reign had been undis-
puted among twice ten million planets.

"You're mad!" One Eye said. "Get out! Our objective is
to conquer this city—not a galaxy."

You did not move. Why did the guards not act then?
Why did not One Eye shoot you down before you had begun
your task?

"This civil war you wage here is fruitless," you said.
"What are you fighting for? A city. The next street! A
powerhouse! These are spoils fit only for scavengers. I
offer you the wealth of Yinnisfar!"

One Eye stood up, showing his teeth. The unkempt hair
on his neck rose like prickles. His leather cheeks turned
mauve. He jerked up his fuser and thrust it toward your
face. You did nothing; there was nothing you needed to do.
Confounded, One Eye sat down again. He had not met such
relentless indifference to threats before, and was impressed.
"Owlenj is only a poor planet with a long history of op-
pression," he muttered. "But it is my world. I have to fight
for it and the people on it, to protect their rights and lib-
erties. I admit that a man of my tactical ability deserves a
better command; possibly when we've brought this city to
its knees. . . ."

Because time was on your side, you had patience. Because you had patience, you listened to One Eye. His talk
was at once grandiose and petty; he spoke largely of the triumph of human rights and narrowly of the shortage of

trained soldiers. He wanted heaven on earth, but he was a platoon short.

He was a man who won respect from his fellows—or fear, if not respect. Yet his principles had been old-fashioned a million millennia ago, before the beginnings of space travel. They had worn wafer thin, used over and over again by countless petty generals: the need for force, the abolition of injustice, the belief that right would win through. You listened with a chill pity, aware that the age-old and majestic intricacies of the Self-perpetuating War had shrunk to this pocket of trouble on Owlenj.

When he stopped orating, you told One Eye your plan for conquering Yinnisfar. You told him that living on Owlenj, on the cold rim of the Galaxy, he could have no idea of the richness of those central worlds; that all the fables the children of Owlenj learned in their meager beds did not convey one-tenth of the wealth of the Suzerain of Yinnisfar; that every man there had his destiny and happiness guarded imperishably.

"Well, we were always underprivileged out here," growled One Eye. "What can anyone here do against the power of the Region?"

So you told him, unsmilingly, that there was one aspect in which Yinnisfar was inferior; it could not, in all its systems, command a general who displayed the sagacity and fearlessness that One Eye was renowned for; its peoples had lost their old lusty arrogance and had declined into mere reverie-begetters.

"All that is so," One Eye admitted reluctantly, "though I have never cared to say so myself. They are a decadent lot!"

"Decadent!" you exclaimed. "They are decadent beyond all belief. They hang like a giant overripe fruit, waiting to drop and splash."

"You really think so?"

"Listen. How long has there been peace throughout the Galaxy—except, of course, for your little difference of opinion here? For millions of years, is that not so? Is it not so peaceful that even interstellar trade has dwindled almost to nothing? I tell you, my friend, the mighty nations of the stars have nodded off to sleep! Their warriors, their technicians, have been untested for generations. Their science rusts beneath a pool of complacency!"

Now you had One Eye on his feet again. This time he was

yours, the first of your list of conquests. He let out a roar of excitement.

"By Thraldemener, it is as you say!" he shouted. "They wouldn't know how to fight. They are degenerate! Come, there is no time to be lost. We will begin the liberation of the peoples of Yinnisfar tomorrow, my friend. Why couldn't I have thought of the idea myself?"

"Wait!" you said. You touched his tattered sleeve as he came around the desk; he felt something of your vitality course through him, and waited obediently. "If Owlenj is to conquer, it must be united. Your forces are not sufficient in themselves to match the dying might of the Region. The civil war must end."

At this One Eye frowned, looked uncertain. Above all else he had wanted to reduce this little city to ashes.

"You can't stop a civil war just like that," he protested.

"You and I go and see the enemy commander," you said.

And although he protested and swore, that was what you and One Eye did.

Treading carefully over the debris, you left by what had been the West Gate and came to the improvised shields of lead and sand which marked One Eye's present forward position. Here One Eye began to argue again; you silenced him. With one man to accompany you and bear the white flag of truce, you put on a radiation suit as One Eye had done and climbed out into the street.

This had once been a fine avenue. Now the tall exoquag trees were splintered like bone, and the fronts of many buildings demolished. Several robotanks lay locked together on the scarred pavements. Nothing moved. But as you walked, you must have been aware of the unseen eyes of the enemy watching you behind their leveled sights.

At the top of the avenue, a mechanical voice halted you and asked you what you wanted. When its attendant echoes had gone chattering away among the ruins, One Eye bellowed out his name and demanded to see the enemy general.

Within two minutes, a transparent disk using beamed power dropped out of the sky. A door slid open and the mechanical voice shouted, "Please get in."

Entering with your two companions, you were at once lifted to a height just above the rooftops. The disk flicked two blocks to the north before sinking again. The door opened and you climbed out.

3

You were in a slaughter yard. No animals were here now, although a wall with a line of fuser marks heart-high showed that the place had not entirely abandoned its ancient purposes.

Two captains met you under a white flag. They saluted One Eye and led you out of the yard, down a deep ramp. You descended to a part of the old-fashioned pneumatic running under the city, where you removed your radiation suit. Here a maze of new corridors had been constructed; down one of them you were led until a white-painted door was reached. The grim captains indicated you were to go in.

You entered.

"Well, you traitor, what makes you think you will leave here alive?" the enemy general asked One Eye. His uniform was trim, if worn, his eyes had a quelling fire to them; he walked as true soldiers have walked since time immemorial —as if the disks of his backbone had all been welded together. And Welded had a little mustache, which now bristled with triumph at the sight of his foe.

Temporarily forgetting all but his old feud, One Eye advanced as if he would tear that mustache from the other's upper lip.

"Shake hands, you two," you said impatiently. "Come to terms immediately. The sooner arrangements are made, the better."

Welded looked at you for the first time; he seemed instantly to comprehend that it was you rather than One Eye with whom he had to deal. Welded was an intelligent man. Instantly, he was ice cold; his voice ground straight off a glacier.

"I have no idea who you are, fellow," he said, "but if I have any suspicion of impertinence from you, I'll have you beamed. With your friend here I must be more careful —his head is destined for the city gate. You are entirely expendable."

"On that I reserve my own opinion," you said. "We do not come here to bandy threats but to make you an offer. If you are prepared to listen, listen now."

In the scale of emotions, there is a stage beyond fury where fury cools, and a stage beyond anger where it merges into fear. As Welded reached this point, he stiffened as if he would snap. He could say nothing. You began to talk of Yinnisfar.

Welded was a harder man to deal with than his enemy, more seasoned, more sure of himself. Though a faint, concupiscent smile curled his lip when you spoke of the richness of the Region, he never unbent. When you had finished, he spoke.

"Are you a native of Owlenj, stranger?" he asked.

"No," you said.

"What is your world, stranger?"

"It is a planet beyond the Galaxy."

"There is nothing between the galaxies. What is the name of the world of yours, stranger?"

"It is unnamed," you said.

Now Welded snapped a finger angrily.

"You have an odd way of trying to win my confidence," he said. "What do the inhabitants of your world call it?"

"There are no inhabitants," you said. "I am the first. It is unnamed because I have not named it."

"Then I will name it," Welded snarled. "I name it Lies! All Lies! Every word a lie! You are a spy from distant Yinnisfar, a dupe, an assassin! Guards!"

As he shouted, he wrenched a fuser from its holster. One Eye kicked out, caught Welded's wrist with the toe of his boot, and sent the weapon flying across the room.

"Listen, you lunatic!" he roared at Welded. "Would you kill this man who offers us so much? Suppose he is a spy from Yinnisfar—would that not make him the ideal man to lead us back there? We need not trust him. Let us seize the advantage of having him in our hands!"

Even while One Eye was speaking, the ceiling had lifted three feet; through the widening gap, armed men catapulted themselves into the room, pinning you and the rebel leader into different corners. In no time, you were enmeshed in clawed metal nets.

Welded stayed them with a raised hand.

"There is a grain of truth in what you say," he admitted reluctantly. "Guards, leave us. We will talk."

Two hours later, when orderlies brought in wine for you and the commanders, the arguing was over and plans were being discussed. By tacit agreement, the question of your origin was abandoned; both men had decided that wherever you came from it was not from the Region of Yinnisfar. No one from that vast empire had bothered with the outer rim of the Galaxy for millennia.

"I came to you," you told them, "because this is one of the few planets near my world on which any form of military organization still survives."

At that they were flattered. They failed to see that you regarded them merely as remnants of an outdated creed. The only advantage of a military organization over any other, from your point of view, was its ability to get into action without inordinate delay.

Two hours later still, when one of Welded's orderlies entered with food, Welded was just making the last of numerous calls to the garrisons of Owlenj.

"How many interstellar vessels do you hold that can be put into active service at once?" he asked into the speaker. "Yes, all told. . . . I see: fifteen. How many of those are light-drive? . . . Only five. What type are those five?"

He wrote the answers down, reading them out as he did so, for your benefit and One Eye's.

"One freighter, one liner converted to military use, one trooper and two invaders. Good. Now give me their tonnages."

He wrote the tonnages down, scowled, nodded, and said with authoritative sharpness to the unseen commander, "Excellent. You will receive instructions in the morning as regards fueling and equipping of those five ships. As for the other ten, get your electronics arm on them immediately. I want them equipped with light-drive and ready to bust vacuum within forty-eight hours. Is that understood? . . . And please confine all your men to camp until further orders. Is that understood? . . . Good. Any queries? . . . I leave it all to your ingenuity, commander. Good night. A jolt in the teeth for him," Welded said with satisfaction as he signed off.

For the first time, he regarded the orderly who had brought in the food.

"Is the general cease fire being obeyed?" he demanded.

"Yes, sir," the orderly said. "The people are dancing in the streets."

"We'll give them something to dance about soon," Welded said, rubbing his hands. He turned to One Eye, who was juggling with pieces of paper.

"What's our strength?" he asked.

"Depends how many of these light-drive conversion craft actually materialize."

"With our present shortage of men and materials, say fifty per cent," Welded said.

"Right." One Eye scanned his one eye over the sheet of figures.

"Including my own fleets, say a hundred and ten starships, about two-thirds of which will be military."

They looked at each other briefly. Provincial though they were, the number still sounded faintly small.

"It is ample," you said confidently.

They turned to the formidable problem of rations. The fleet could reckon on being vacuum-borne for two weeks before reaching the margins of the Region; another two and a half weeks to reach the heart; another three days to the pivotal world of Yinnisfar itself.

"And that allows no time for delay caused by evasive action or battle," Welded said.

"They may capitulate before we reach Yinnisfar itself," you said.

"We must have a safety margin," Welded insisted. "Let's call it a six-week journey, eh? And we'll be five and a half thousand strong. . . ." He shook his head. "We can cope with air supply. The calorie intake is going to be the snag. Those men'll eat their heads off in that time; there's just not that amount of food on all Owlenj. Deep freeze is our only answer. Everyone below the rank of major not on essential ship's crew travels frozen. Get me Medical, orderly. I want to speak to the physician general."

The orderly hastened to obey.

"What's next?" Welded asked. He was beginning to enjoy himself.

"Weapons," One Eye said. "First, fissionable material. My forces can't help much there. Our stocks happen to be lower than usual."

"Here's a report on our holdings as of last week," Welded said, tossing a stereoed list over. "Stocks are meager, I'm afraid."

You glanced at the list over One Eye's shoulder.

"It is ample," you said encouragingly.

4

At first it must have seemed as if the scheme might succeed. Again the feeling must have assailed you that you lived in an unlikely dream whose scenery you could puncture with a finger, as you sat in the flagship with the two commanders. You had no nerves; you did not worry. Welded and One Eye, in their individual ways, both showed strain now that they were embarked on the journey. The captain of the ship, Fleet Commander Prim, had to endure much quiet nagging.

The early days passed uneventfully. Beyond the ports, space hung becalmed, its blazing stars mere specks in the distance, its ancient splendors nothing more than points to navigate by. The other ships were not visible to the unaided eye; the flagship might have been traveling alone. When they had blasted from Owlenj, the ships in the invasion fleet had numbered 117; by the end of the first week five had had to give up and limp home again, their too hastily contrived light-drives burned out. It would take them, under normal thrust, half a year to regain port; by then, their crews would be asphyxiated or the survivors breathing the oxygen of murdered men. The rest of the fleet sailed on, holds full of soldiers in suspended animation, all neatly stacked and racked like bottles.

They had been vacuum-borne sixteen days, and were past those stars generally regarded as outposts of the empire of Yinnisfar, when they were first challenged.

"A station calling itself Camoens II RST225," the communications chief reported, "asks us why we have passed Koramandel Tangent Ten without identifying ourselves."

"Let it keep on calling," you said.

Other challenges were received and left unanswered. The fleet stayed silent as it startled to life the worlds about it. Communications began to intercept messages of alarm and warning between planetary stations.

"Galcondar Saber calling Rolf 158. Unidentified craft due to pass you on course 99GY4281 at 07.1430 Gal. approx—"

"Acrostic 1 to Schiaparelli Base. Look out and report on fleet now entering Home Sector Paradise 014—"

"Peik-pi-Koing Astronomical to Droxy Pylon. Unidentified ships numbering 130 approx now crossing Scanning Area. Code Diamond Index Diamond Oh Nine—"

"All stations on Ishrail Link Two. Procedure BAB Nine One into operation immediately—"

One Eye snorted his contempt.

"We've certainly set these provincial globes in a flutter," he said.

As the hours passed, he grew less easy. Space, almost silent a watch ago, now became murmurous with voices; soon the murmur grew into a babel. The note of curiosity, at first indicating little more than mild interest, showed a corresponding rise through irritation into alarm.

"Perhaps we ought to answer them," One Eye suggested. "Couldn't we spin them some tale to keep them quiet? Tell them we are going to pay homage, or something?"

"You need have no worry about the messages we can understand," Prim said. "We are picking up several in code now; they are the ones which should cause us most concern."

"Haven't we some sort of yarn to keep them quiet?" One Eye repeated, appealing to you.

You were looking out into the darkness, almost as if you could see through the veil of it, almost as if you expected to see the messages flashing like comets before the ports.

"The truth will emerge," you said, without turning around.

Two days later, the parasond picked up the first ship they had detected since leaving Owlenj.

"It *can't* be a ship!" the communications chief was saying, waving a flimog with the report on it.

"But it must be," his sub almost pleaded. "Look at its course: you plotted it back yourself! It's definitely turning. What but a ship could maneuver?"

"It *can't* be a ship!" the chief repeated.

"Why can't it be a ship?" Prim asked.

"Beg pardon, sir, but the thing's at least thirty miles long."

After a silence, One Eye asked, "Which way's it coming?"

The sub spoke up. He alone seemed delighted at the fish they had caught on their screen. "It has turned since we had it under observation through thirty to thirty-two degrees northerly from a course about due nor'-nor'west with respect to galactic quadrature."

One Eye grasped the back of the sub's couch as if it were the sub's neck.

"What I want to know," he growled, "is if it's going away or coming toward us."

"Neither," said the sub, looking at the screen again. "It now seems to have finished turning and is moving along a course which is . . . at ninety degrees to ours."

"Any signal from it?" Prim asked.

"Nothing."

"Put a shot across its bows," One Eye suggested.

"You are not groveling along the streets of Owlenj now, taking pot shots at all and sundry. Let it go!"

One Eye turned angrily, to find Welded there. The latter had come up on the bridge early. He stood and watched the blob fade from the parasond screen before he spoke again. Then, beckoning One Eye aside and looking to make sure you were not then present on the bridge, he said in a low voice, "My friend, I have something to confess to you."

He looked anxiously and with distaste at One Eye's whiskery countenance before continuing.

"My early fears are coming back to me," he said. "You know I am a man of courage, but even a hero does wisely to be afraid at times. Every hour we dive deeper into a hornet's nest; do you realize that? Why, we are only two and a half weeks from Yinnisfar itself! I cannot sleep for asking myself if we are not running into something from which there will be no escape."

Reluctant as he was to agree with an old enemy, One Eye could not miss this chance of confiding his own anxieties.

"Ships thirty miles long!" he exclaimed.

Nodding mysteriously, Welded persuaded the other to come down to his cabin before he would say more. Then he thumped the bulkhead.

"Only a watch's journey from here," he said, thumping again for emphasis, "are many rich planets. They will be as plunder-worthy as the planets in the heart of the Region—but less well guarded. Can't you just picture them at this very moment: loaded with plump semiblondes with rings on every finger, and fat little men dallying with big bank accounts? They're wide open! Defenseless! Why go on to Yinnisfar, where undoubtedly we shall meet with resistance? Why not stop here, plunder what we can, and get back to Owlenj while the going's good?"

One Eye hesitated, his lip thrust out. He liked the suggestion every bit as much as his ex-enemy had expected he would. But there was one major obstacle.

"*He*'s set his heart on getting to Yinnisfar itself."

"Yes! I think we've put up with *him* long enough," Welded replied.

They did not need to mention your name. When away from the aura of your presence, their misgivings about you were mutual. Welded crossed to a cupboard, taking out a small and tightly stoppered bottle.

"This should solve *that* problem," he said.

It contained a deadly venom; to smell one drop of it a yard away would give a man headaches for a week.

"Something to flavor his wine with tonight," Welded said.

5

When the wine went round the captain's table after dinner, One Eye accepted his glass but could not drink. He felt sick with suspense, and with the sickness went a loathing for Welded; not only did he disapprove of poisoning, as a devious method of killing, but he understood clearly that the little bottle held more than enough to spare for him, too, should Welded feel like disposing of all his opposition at once.

You had no such qualms. You took your glass when it was filled, toasted, as you did every night, the success of the expedition, and drained down the wine.

"This wine tastes flat," you said. "We will stock up with better vintages on Yinnisfar!"

Everyone around the table laughed with you, except for One Eye; the muscles of his face contorted. He could not even force himself to look at Welded.

"What did you make of the thirty-mile-long object we sighted earlier?" Prim asked you, taking his wine at a more sedate pace.

"It was a Yinnisfar ship," you said easily. "But don't worry about it. Evolution will take care of it, just as evolution took care of the prehistoric monsters that once roved Owlenj and other planets."

The captain spread his hands.

"For a practical man, that seems a strangely unpractical remark," he said. "Evolution is one thing, superships quite another."

"Only if you forget that evolution is nature's scientific method, and starships, not being organic creatures, are a part of man's evolution. And man himself is but a part of nature's scientific method."

"I trust you don't imagine, at this late date in time, that man is not the end product of evolution?" he asked you. "We are constantly being told that the Galaxy is too old for anything but final extinction."

"I imagine nothing," you told him pleasantly. "But remember—what triumphs ultimately is something too vast for comprehension—yours or mine."

You stood up, and the others followed suit. Soon the dining room was empty except for two very puzzled conspirators.

For just over four weeks, the Owlenj fleet had been vacuum-borne. Now the craft were deep within the star-clotted heart of the Galaxy. Suns which carried as an incidental burden hundreds of millions of years of the histories and myths of man burned on all sides like funeral torches. The graveyard air was reinforced by silence over all wave bands, the chatter of alarmed planets had died away to nothing.

"They're waiting for us!" One Eye exclaimed, not for the first time. He lived on the bridge of the flagship now, staring for hours at a time at the seemingly motionless spectacle of the universe.

Much to the captain's unstated disapproval, the bridge had also become Welded's living quarters. He spent most of the time lying on his bed with a fuser under his pillow, and never looked out of the ports.

You came frequently to the bridge, but seldom spoke to the two. You were detached; it might have been all a dream. Yet, for all that, you were at times noticeably impatient, speaking abruptly, sometimes clicking your fingers in suppressed irritation, almost as if you wished to wake from the tedium of your sleep.

Only Fleet Commander Prim remained completely unchanged. The routine of command stayed him. He seemed to have absorbed all the confidence One Eye and Welded had lost.

"We shall ground on Yinnisfar in six days," he said to you. "Is it possible they intend to offer us no resistance?"

"It is possible to think up excellent reasons for their nonresistance," you said. "Owlenj has been isolated from the Federation for generations and has little knowledge of current intellectual attitudes within the Region. They may all be pacifists, eager to prove their faith. Or, at the other end of the scale, their military hierarchy, without war to thin its ranks, may already have collapsed under our unexpected pressure. It's all speculation—"

At that second, the parasond exploded. An icy clatter rang along the floor as ruptured metal and glass showered out of the panel, while gusts of acrid smoke settled like mesh over the bridge. A babble of voices broke out.

"Get the communications chief," Prim barked, but the chief was already on the job, calling over the intercom for a stretcher party and the electronics crew.

Welded was inspecting the damage, fanning away smoke, which still siphoned out of a red-hot crater in the panels. His spine arched as tensely as a prestressed girder.

"Look!" called One Eye. The hysterical edge to his voice was so compelling that even in this moment of crisis every eye present swiveled to where his finger pointed. Out, out they stared into the hard pageant of night beyond the ports. Their eyes had to probe and focus before they saw.

Flies. Flies, rising in a cloud from a dark stream on whose surface sunlight glittered, so that between dark and light the insects were almost lost to view. But the stream was space itself and the glitter a spangle of suns, and the flies spread across them—a cloud of ships. The ancient forces of Yinnisfar were rising to the attack.

6

"You can't count them!" One Eye said, glaring aghast at the swarm of ships. "There must be thousands. *They* blew out the instrument panel; it was a sort of warning. By Pla and To, they'll blow us into eternity at any moment!"

Turning on a heel, he crossed the promenade and confronted you.

"You brought us into this!" he shouted. "What are you going to do to get us away? How do we save ourselves?"

"Leave that to the captain and be silent," you said. You moved away before he touched you and stood by the captain.

The short wave was unimpaired, and he spoke rapidly to the squadron leaders of his fleet. On a live schematic above his head, the results of those orders immediately became apparent. The Owlenjan fleet was deploying into its individual squadrons, spreading into a fan parsecs wide. They moved toward the curtain of flies like an opening hand. At maximum speed they moved, straight for the enemy navies.

"They're too ready for us," Prim said to you out of the corner of his dry mouth. "There aren't enough of us to be effective. It's nothing but suicide."

"What else do you suggest?" you asked him.

"If every ship made for a planet, orbited it, held it under threat of demolition— No, they'd pick us off one by one . . ." He shook his head. "This is the only possible way," he said quietly, again turning all his attention to the maneuver.

Further talk was impossible. The waiting ships and the handful of charging starcraft slid together. The gulf between them suddenly became trellised with blue flame—electric, blinding. Square links of force opened and shut like champing mouths. Whatever its power source, the drain must have been phenomenal, consuming the basic energies of space itself.

The Owlenjan ships found themselves on the defensive before evasion was more than a panicky thought. That chopping trellis flared before their ports, snapped, was gone, flared and snapped again, bathing every bridge in its eccentric luminance, dazzling, consuming. It was the last light thousands of eyes ever saw. The ships on which those blue jaws closed burned magnesium-bright; they burned, then sagged into limbo, leeched of life.

But the invaders were tearing through space at formidable speeds. Nor was the terrifying trellis properly in phase; whoever controlled it could not control its precise adjustment. Its scissor action was too slow—many ships hurtled through its interstices and into the ranks of the Yinnisfar fleet.

A glance at the schematic showed Prim he had only about forty ships left, raggedly out of formation.

"Superfusers—fire!" he roared.

No one in that immense melee of armor had ever been in a space battle before. The Galaxy in its tired old age had long since hung up its swords. Of all the astute minds following the rapid interplay of strategy, Prim's was the quickest to seize advantage. The mighty ranks of Yinnisfar had placed too much reliance on their trellis device; they were temporarily numbed to find survivors on their side of it. Owlenj shook them out of their numbness.

Sunbursts of superfusers cascaded among them, leaping and feeding from ship to ship, coruscating with cosmu energy, while the attackers plunged through their devastated ranks and were away. The Yinnisfar vessels were also in rapid movement. In no time they had dispersed, safe from the fusion center, where twenty score of their sister ships had perished.

"We're through!" you said. "On to Yinnisfar itself. It will ransom our safety!"

The enemy fleet was not so easily outdistanced, however. Several units were already overtaking the invaders at staggering velocity. Among them was the thirty-mile-long craft they had sighted some days earlier.

"And there are three more like it!" Welder yelled from his position at the ports "Look! How can anything travel that fast?"

Prim wrenched the flagship into a spin south. They altered course just in time; the overtakers launched a black mass like smoke directly ahead of their old position. The smoke was molecularized ceetee, capable of riddling the flagship like a moth in a carpet, leaving it mere gravel over the spaceways. In this maneuver, sight of the four giant vessels was lost. Then they spun into sight again, and with mind-wrenching turns formed the four points of an enormous square ahead of the flagship.

"No human could stand G's like that. They are robot-controlled," you said, gripped by the fascination of battle.

"And *they* put out the trellis screen!" Prim said. It was a flash of inspiration, shortly to be proved correct. He turned and barked orders at bombardment, telling them to hit the giants at any cost. By now the flagship was on its own, the rest of its company disintegrated or scattered far away.

The four giants were in position. Again the hellish blue pattern scissored across the flagship's course. Prim had no time to swerve away—they racketed toward the dazzling pattern. At the last moment, bombardment fired a superfuser dead ahead.

Superfuser and trellis met.

The two insensate energies clawed each other like vast beasts of prey. Instead of spreading its usual explosion, the fusion climbed the writhing squares of trellis, gobbling as it mounted. At the center it left a widening circle of nothingness, through which the flagship shot unharmed. It climbed to the trellis corners, barbed fire-devouring fire. It reached the four giant vessels.

Just for a moment they remained intact, each radiating a three-dimensional rainbow which flickered magically up and down the spectrum and was visible hundreds of light years away. Then that blinding beauty fused, the four rainbow orbs merged and became antilight. They sucked, guttered and went out—and a great gap in the nothingness of the universe appeared and spread. The ineluctable fabric of space itself was being devoured.

Several Yinnisfar ships were engulfed in this cataclysm. The flagship was spared no time to rejoice. The moment of its greatest triumph was also the moment of its destruction. A translucent globe from an enemy destroyer caught its dorsal vane.

Like an electronic monster, the globe spread tentacles of light and engulfed the flagship.

Prim swore furiously.

"Nothing responds any more," he said, dropping his hands to his sides.

It was doubtful if anyone heard him. A continuous sizzle filled their ears while their body electricity jumped in protest at what was taking place. The scene was rendered in unforgettable hues of orange and black, as the light penetrated everything. Faces, clothes, floor, instruments, all were ravaged.

Then it was over, that moment of near madness. They were left in darkness, only pale starlight touching their faces. Prim staggered for the controls. He swept his hand wildly over banks of instruments. All were dead.

"We're finished!" he announced. "Not a whisper of life anywhere. Even the air purifier is finished."

He sank down, covering his face with his hands. For a while no one spoke; all were emotionally drained by the apocalyptic rigors of battle, the sag of defeat.

"They must be chivalrous on Yinnisfar," you said at length. "They will have some residual code of battle. They will come and take us. We shall be honorably treated."

Welded said harshly from a corner, "You still find room for cockiness! We ought to destroy you now."

"Let's kill him," One Eye said, but made no move. They were all just lumps against the wall of starlight, lumps that spoke without relevance.

"I only feel relaxed," you said. "The battle is over. We have lost honorably. Look at your captain here, half-dead with fatigue. He fought well, resourcefully. No blame lies with him that we lost the gamble. Now he can sit back without remorse—and we can do the same—knowing the future is not in our hands. Soon they will be here to collect us and give us an honorable trial on Yinnisfar."

The others made you no answer.

7

The air was growing foul when the emissaries of Yinnisfar arrived, as you had predicted. They cut their way rapidly through the hull, rounded up all of the dazed men aboard and transferred them to their own ship. Full speed was then made toward Yinnisfar. The flagship was left to its own ruined devices.

You had been given a separate room with Prim, One Eye, and Welded. The latter two had been quite drained of all life

by the magnitude of recent events. They sat together now like
a pair of dummies, not speaking. Prim was in better shape,
but reaction had hit him now, and he lay shaking on a couch.
So you alone stood by the port and took in the spectacle as
Yinnisfar approached.

The planet which for so long had played such a prominent
role in the Galaxy was a curious spectacle at this late date
in its history. About its equator circled two splendid rings,
one beyond the other. Of these rings, the first was natural and
consisted of the debris of Luna, disintegrated when an antique
craft embedded in Iri had suddenly exploded. The other ring
was nothing more or less than a scrapyard. Breaking up
spaceships on the ground had been forbidden ages ago on
Yinnisfar, where piles of rusting metal were considered un-
sightly; instead, every fragment of scrap was thrown into the
orbit of the ring. Over a vast period of time, this ring had
grown until it was fifty miles deep and several hundred wide.
Far from being ugly, it was a thing of beauty, one of the
seventeen wonders of the Galaxy. It gleamed like an array
of countless jewels, every inch of metal polished eternally
by the ceaseless wash of meteoric dust.

When the ship in which you were held landed on the day
side of the planet, the second ring was still faintly visible,
straining like an arch around heaven.

This was Yinnisfar of tears and pleasures, stuffed with
forgotten memories and protracted time.

After some delay, you and the others were disembarked,
transferred to a small surface ship and taken to the Court
of the Highest Suzerain in the city of Nion. The flagship crew
was spirited off in one direction and the troops, still in suspended animation, in another, while you and the three offi-
cers were ushered into a room little bigger than a cubicle.
Here again was more delay. Food was brought, but you
alone were inclined to eat it, supplementing it with supplies
that you carried on your person.

Various dignitaries visited you, most of them departing
gloomily, without speaking. Through a narrow window you
looked out onto a courtyard, brightened in one corner by a
beautiful flowering jenny-merit. Groups of men and women
stood about aimlessly, and no face was without its stamp of
worry. Counselors walked as if climbing a dark stair. It became clear that some grave crisis pended; its threat hung
almost tangibly over the whole court.

Finally and unexpectedly, an order reached your guards.

With a flurry of excitement you and the three with you were brought into a marble hall of audience and so into the personal presence of the Highest, Suzerain Inherit of Yinnisfar and the Region of Yinnisfar.

He was a pale man, dressed austerely in dark satins. He reclined on a couch. His features were leached, yet his eyes spoke of supreme intelligence and his voice was firm. Though his general pose suggested lethargy, his head was carried with an alertness that did not escape your attention.

He looked you over in leisurely fashion, weighing each of your group in turn, and finally addressed you as the leader. He spoke without preamble.

"You barbarians, by the folly of your actions, have wrought havoc."

You bowed and said with irony, "We regret it if we disturbed the great empire of Yinnisfar."

"Pah! I do not refer to the empire." He waved his hand as if the empire were a bauble, beneath his interest. "I refer to the cosmos itself, by whose grace we all exist. The forces of nature have become unknit."

You looked at him interrogatively, saying nothing.

"Let me explain the fate which now threatens," the Highest said, "in the hope you may die knowing a little of what you have done. Our Galaxy is old beyond imagining; philosophers, theologians and scientists combine to tell us that its duration, vast but not infinite, is nearing an end."

"The rumor has circulated," you murmured.

"I am pleased to hear that wisdom travels. We have learned in these last few hours that the Galaxy—like an old curtain crumbling under its own weight—is dissolving; that this, in fact, is the end of all things, of past and future, and of all men."

He paused in vain, to watch for any shadows of alarm crossing your face, then continued, ignoring the frightened responses of your fellow captives.

"Peace has reigned in the Region for millennia. But when we learned your fleet was coming with hostile intent, our ancient ships and engines of attack—unused since the breakdown of the Self-perpetuating War—were resurrected. Systems of production, schemes of battle, organizations of fighting men—all had to be resurrected from the long-dead past. It required haste such as we have never known, and regimentation such as we detest."

"That's worth a cheer anyway," One Eye said, with an attempt at courage.

The Highest regarded him for a moment before continuing.

"We found, in our hurried search for weapons to use against you, one which was invented eons ago and never used. It was considered dangerous, since it harnessed the electrogravitic forces of the complex of space itself. Four gigantic machines called turbulators activated this force; they were the four ships you destroyed."

"We saw one of them on the margins of the Region days ago," Prim said. He had been following the Highest with excitement, enthralled by his description of a gigantic military organization grinding into action.

"The four turbulators had to be called from the distant quarters of the Region, where our ancestors had discarded them," the Highest explained. "They were stationed across the course of your fleet with the results that you saw. The trellis is the basic pattern of creation itself. By ill chance you destroyed it, or rather caused it to begin consuming itself. Our scientists suggest that such is the antiquity of our Galaxy, it no longer retains its ancient stability. Although the process is invisible, the disintegration you began continues—is spreading rapidly, in fact—and nothing known can stop it."

Prim staggered back, as if struck.

The Highest stared at you, expecting a reply. As if uncertain for the first time, you looked searchingly at One Eye and the others; they stared blankly ahead, too absorbed with the prospect of catastrophe to notice you.

"Your scientists are to be congratulated," you said. "They are late with their discovery of instability, but at least they have found it out for themselves. It is a catastrophe my friends here and I did not begin; it began long ago, and it was about that that I came to Yinnisfar to tell them—and you."

For the first time, the Highest showed emotion. He rose from the couch, clutching its back fiercely. "You impertinent barbarian, you came here to rape and loot and pillage. What do you know of these matters?"

"I came here to announce the end of things," you told him. "How I arrived, whether as captive or victor, was no concern of mine, so long as the peoples of every world had been roused to know of my coming. That was why I staged the invasion; such a thing is easily done, provided you can read and provoke the few basic human passions. If I had come here alone, who would have known or cared? As it is, the whole Galaxy has its myriad eyes open and I focused them on Yinnisfar. They may die knowing the truth."

"Indeed?" The Highest raised an imperial eyebrow. "Before I have you erased, perhaps you might care to tell me about this truth over which you have gone to such trouble?"

"By all means," you replied. "Perhaps you would care for a demonstration first?"

But the Highest brushed the suggestion aside, snapping his fingers. "You are a braggart!" he said energetically. "You waste my time, and there is little enough left. Guards!"

The guards advanced in a half-circle, eager at an unprecedented chance to try their art on living flesh.

"This is the sort of demonstration I had in mind," you said, turning to meet them.

Fourteen men comprised the guard. Their uniforms were laced, epauleted and braided; but their antique swords looked functional.

Without hesitation you advanced toward the nearest soldier. He, with equal decision, brought down his sword with a heavy blow at your head. You flung up your arm and caught the blade full on it.

The sword rang and crumbled into bits, as if turned to dust. The swordsman fell back in alarm.

The other guards were on you, thrusting and slicing. Their swords crumpled and snapped against you; not one but wrecked itself against your body.

When it was realized that you had—how would they think of it?—a secret power, they fell back. You saw then that from a balcony the snout of a machine was trained on you.

"Before you are annihilated," the Highest said, glancing pointedly up at the balcony, "tell me what form of trickery this is."

"Try out your own trick first," you suggested. To hasten matters, you stepped toward the Highest. You had taken perhaps two paces before the machine on the balcony burst into action. A fusillade of beta pellets screamed toward you, only ⌐ fall uselessly to the ground at your feet.

⌐t last the Highest seemed daunted.

"Who are you? Where do you come from?"

"That is what I wish to tell you," you said. "What I have to say must go out to every one of your people; when a great history ends, it ends most fittingly with everyone knowing why; a man who perishes without reason makes a mockery of all he stands for.

"I come from a new world beyond this Galaxy—new because there the process of creation still goes on. New galaxies are forming out of the fathomless night, rising out of the margins of emptiness. My planet is new, and I am the first man upon it; it is nameless."

Welded said, "So all you told me back on Owlenj was true?"

"Certainly," you said. You did not bother to tell him how you had learned to pilot the dead Shouter's ship. You turned instead to Prim. "Do you recall a conversation we once had about evolution? You claimed that man was its ultimate product."

Prim nodded.

"Man is evolution's fittest fruit—in *this* Galaxy," you told him. You looked at the Highest, at Welded, at One Eye. Without smiling, you said, "You are evolution's highest flowering here. Think of the multitudes of experiments nature undertook before evolving you. She started with amino acids, then the amoeba, a simple cell. . . . She was like a child at school then, but all this while she has been learning. I use analogies without subscribing to the pathetic fallacy, understand. Many of her experiments—even late ones like the sentient vagabond cells—are failures; man, on the whole, is her best so far.

"In the new galaxy from which I come, she *begins* with man. I am the earliest, most primitive form of life in my galaxy—the new amoeba!"

You went on to tell them how in you radical changes had been made; you were, in truth, a different species. Your waste system was fundamentally altered. Your digestive processes had been changed. Genetically, not only were the old characteristics transferable from one generation to another; walking and language genes insured that those simple human skills were also inheritable. The psychological basis of your mind had been improved; much of man's old random emotionalism had been eliminated entirely. Yet you had a range of altruism and identity with things surpassing man's capabilities.

The Highest heard you out in silence and then said, "As the first of your—ah—species, how is it you can know so much about yourself?"

You smiled. It seemed a simple question.

"Because all our other improvements are merely in some way a modification of the pattern used in man's designing, I have in addition one priceless gift: an awareness not only of my psychological actions—thoughts, if you will—but of my physiological ones. I can control the working of my every enzyme, see into each last blood cell. I am integrated as you could never be. For instance, diseases can never touch me; I should recognize and check each at its inception. Nor do I freeze in a moment of crisis and get taken over by automatic reflexes; knowing myself, I am, quite literally, my own master. Though you have mastered your environment, you have never mastered yourselves."

8

The Highest came down from his dais.

"There was enough to worry about before you arrived," he said. "Though I have lived five centuries, I am as a child again. Why, you must feel quite the superman on Yinnisfar!"

The derision in his tone pricked.

"Didn't you understand me?" you flashed. "In my world, I rank as the amoeba. Should that make me proud? As to what supersedes me—"

The Highest raised a manicured hand, and said, "I concede your point; you are suitably humble about your own might."

"What's the good of all this talk?" It was One Eye. He had stood helplessly by with Welded and Prim, his mind filled with fruitless plots of escape. Now he came up to you with a mixture of defiance and cajolery.

"You got us here, you can get us back," he said. "And let's not wait. Get us back to Owlenj if you're such a superman."

You shook your head.

"You'd be no better off on Owlenj, of that I can assure you," you told him. "I'm sorry you had to be involved in this, but it's been no worse for you than hiding out in the ruins of a city. And I'm no superman—"

"No superman!" One Eye said angrily. He turned to the Highest and exclaimed, "No superman, he says. Yet he drank down enough poison for an army, he fended off those swords—you saw him!—he withstood a bombardment just then—"

"Listen to me!" you interrupted. "Those things belonged to a different principle. Watch this!"

You walked over to a wall. It was built of solid blocks of marble, polished and selected for their delicate patterning. You placed one hand with extended fingers upon it and pushed; when you withdrew your hand, five short tunnels had been pierced in the marble.

It was a simple demonstration. They were properly impressed.

You wiped your hand and returned to them, but they shuffled away from you, their lips pale.

"Yet I am no stronger than you," you told them. "The difference is only this: that I come from a freshly created world, new minted by the inexorable processes of continuous creation. And you—come from an old world. Think of your Galaxy. How old is it? You do not know exactly, but you know it is incredibly old. The truth is, it is wearing out, as everything wears out in time. Nothing is meant to last. Ask yourself what everything is made of. A tissue of energies which outcrops and becomes matter. That tissue of energy, since the beginning of time, has been running down, wearing thin. All matter, which is composed of it, has worn thin with it. The great magical batteries of your Galaxy are slowing, so all protons and neutrons lose their polarity. Their charges have run low, they cannot combine as they once used to. Steel has not the strength that paper once possessed, wood is water."

Prim interrupted.

"You're trying to deceive us!" he told you in a trembling voice. "It's only *you* who can pierce marble with a finger, or withstand poison, swords, or bombardment. *We* would die! Do you take us for fools?"

"No," you replied. "You would die, as you say. You are composed of the same exhausted nuclei as everything else; that is exactly why you could not detect this process long ago. I can withstand almost anything you have to offer only because the very stuff of which I am made is new. I am the one fresh factor in an exhausted galaxy."

You paused and went over to the Highest. He had become very pale. "This ravening monster we loosed between us out in space—I suppose that merely hastens the exhaustion process?" he asked.

"Yes. The fabric is torn; the gap widens to embrace your island universe."

The Highest closed his eyes. When he raised his lids again, his regard fixed on you with the alertness of a bird.

"Our poisons cannot affect you," he said. "Yet you manage to live among us. How can our food nourish you?"

"I brought my private supply of calories with me when I left my own world. I was not unprepared. I had even to bring oxygen concentrates."

You then told the Highest of the effects your unexhausted air had had on Shouter, the spool-seller, how he had been riddled as if by unseen radiations. And you told him how useful Shouter's microspool library had been.

"An opportunist," the Highest said. "My congratulations to you."

He pulled at his lip and looked, for a moment, almost amused.

"Have you a moment to spare, if the question has meaning any longer? Perhaps the others will excuse us."

Something in his manner had changed. He motioned to you with a sharp gesture and made for a door. What did you do? You took a last look over your shoulder at the desolate group whose function in life had abruptly vanished, gave One Eye a mocking salute and followed.

The Highest walked down a corridor at a pace which belied his earlier languor. He flung open another door and you both emerged onto a balcony overlooking the proud city of Nion. A cool evening wind blew; clouds masked the setting sun. The great panorama of avenue and river lay strangely deserted, from distant spires to the pavements of a nearby concourse. Nothing stirred except a fabric far below in a mansion window.

"How long would this exhaustion process have taken had we not accelerated it?" the Highest asked almost casually, leaning on the rail and looking down.

"It must have worsened for centuries," you told him. "It might have gone on for centuries more. . . ."

You felt a softness for him, and for all men, all the myriads of them, whether they cheated or played fair, loved or hated. All their follies and limitations were forgiven; they were primitives, coming from the dark, fading back into the dark, with a glimpsing of awareness to give poignance.

The Highest took a deep breath of evening.

"It's ending! Now comes the time to adventure into death."
He took another lungful of the darkening wind.

"And you have a ringside seat, my friend. It will indeed be a sight to see. But you must get back before our craft disintegrate. They won't be capable of carrying you much longer."

You said, gently, "Everyone must be told what is happening. That seems imperative."

"I will not forget."

He turned and faced you.

"What impulse brought you here? Nostalgia? Curiosity? Pity? What feelings do you have for—us shadows?"

And what unexpected weakness was it that choked the words in your throat? Why did you turn your face away so that he could not see your eyes?

"I wanted man to be aware of what is happening to him," you said at last. "That much was owed him. I—*we* owed it. You are—our fathers. We are your heirs. . . ."

He touched you gently, asking in a firm voice, "What should be told to the people of the Galaxy?"

You looked out over a city now pricked with lights, and up to the evening sky. You found no comfort there or in yourself.

"Tell them again what a galaxy is," you said. "Don't soften it. They are brave. Explain to them once more that there are galaxies like grains of sand, each galaxy a cosmic laboratory for the blind experiments of nature. Explain to them how little individual lives mean compared to the unknown goals of the race. Tell them—tell them that this laboratory is closing. A newer one, with more modern equipment, is opening just down the street."

"They shall be told," the Highest said, his face a shadow as night fell upon the old city and the stars.

We who have already superseded you record these scenes now in your honor, as you once honored man. REQUIESCAS IN PACE.